MURDER AT THE GORGE

FRANCES EVESHAM

Boldwood

First published in Great Britain in 2020 by Boldwood Books Ltd.

A CIP catalogue record for this book is available from the British Library.

Paperback ISBN 978-1-80048-045-2

Large Print ISBN 978-1-80048-046-9

Ebook ISBN 978-1-80048-048-3

Kindle ISBN 978-1-80048-047-6

Audio CD ISBN 978-1-80048-040-7

MP3 CD ISBN 978-1-80048-041-4

Digital audio download ISBN 978-1-80048-044-5

Boldwood Books Ltd
23 Bowerdean Street
London SW6 3TN
www.boldwoodbooks.com

1

APPLE CAKE

Sand blew fiercely across Exham on Sea beach, slicing into any intrepid walker brave enough to venture out. Max Ramshore shivered, despite the padded jacket he'd zipped right up to his chin. The late-November wind from the sea always found the slightest chink in his clothing. He pulled his beanie lower over his forehead and made a mental note to buy a warmer scarf.

In summer, the eight miles of sand were a delight, the air tangy with ozone and fish and chips, and the beach dotted with cheerful holidaymakers eating ice cream, balancing small children on obliging, mild-tempered donkeys, and helping to build sandcastles.

In winter, the seafront belonged once more to the locals.

Max and Libby were determined, today, to reach the wooden Low Lighthouse. 'I have mixed feelings when I walk here,' Libby said. She pointed. 'Look, that's where I found the first body, lying against one of the wooden legs. It still sends shivers down my spine to remember poor Susie, slumped there like a sack of coal. At least her murder brought us together.'

'Ramshore and Forest, detectives extraordinaire,' Max teased.

'Forest and Ramshore,' Libby insisted, as she always did. No wonder they'd never agreed on a letterhead or logo for their private investigation business, even though it now took up almost as much time as producing her famous cakes and chocolates.

Libby stood by Max's side, watching the two dogs cavorting in the sand. She had a smile on her lips. That smile was almost constant, these days.

Max forgot the cold seeping into his neck, and counted his blessings.

In almost two weeks, they'd be married.

Bear, Max's huge, now rather elderly, Carpathian sheepdog decided an interesting morsel lay just beneath the sand under the lighthouse and dug furiously with giant paws, sand flying in every direction.

'Watch out,' Max shouted, too late, as sand hit him squarely in the left eye. Blinking furiously, trying not to rub the eye, he staggered upwind of Bear just as Shipley, his springer spaniel, dropped a stick twice his own size at Max's feet.

Max's curse was lost in Shipley's excited barking and Libby's shout of laughter. She retrieved the stick and threw it for Shipley to chase.

'Come here,' she told Max, 'let me wash the sand out of your eye.'

His back to the wind, Max let her dribble bottled water from her rucksack into his eye and scrub around it with a tissue. She'd never make a nurse, but he decided the embrace that followed was worth the pain.

'I shall enjoy married life if you look after me like that,' he murmured. 'You're a useful person to have around.'

'For the first aid or the cooking?'

'Both. I'm expecting to sample every single one of the cake recipes in your "Baking at the Beach" books.'

Libby pulled back a little to look into his face, ducking as the breeze hurled more sand their way. '*Baking at the Beach* is a great title, but not a sensible activity in November,' she admitted.

'You can call book three, *Baking in a nice warm kitchen.*'

She laughed. How he loved that sound; a proper, deep chortle. His ex-wife had laughed with an affected noise designed, he was sure, to sound like tinkling bells.

He took Libby's arm, whistling for the dogs. Shipley, who'd recently undergone strict retraining, returned at once, but Bear went on digging.

'Do you think he's getting deaf?' Libby asked. 'He used to come when I called, but lately he's been ignoring me.'

Max studied Bear. 'Hard to say. He's not as young as he used to be and I've noticed he limps a little. Rheumatism, maybe.'

Libby was frowning. 'I know twelve is old for a Carpathian, but I can't imagine life without him. Maybe he needs a visit to the vet? To be checked out?'

'I'll take him, if you'll please agree we can go home now and get out of this wind?'

'Wimp.'

The wind blew them back to Max's Land Rover, parked near the jetty, in half the time it had taken them to reach the lighthouse.

As they flung open the doors and the dogs scrambled on board, Max's phone rang. He shot a glance at the screen and his stomach lurched. Stella. His ex-wife. He hadn't heard from her for years. His finger hovered over the red button for a second, but he knew she'd just call again. Reluctantly, he answered.

'Hello?'

'Max, I need your help. I'm in Bristol. Come and see me. Now.'

Max stared at the phone, stunned into silence.

Libby climbed into the passenger seat. 'Who is it? Business?'

Max croaked into the phone, 'I'll call you back,' ended the call and dropped the phone into his pocket as though it had burned his fingers.

Libby pulled her seat belt tight. 'That was a bit abrupt. You'll frighten customers away. You could take a lesson from the way Mandy answers the phone at work. Butter wouldn't melt in her mouth, these days.'

She chattered happily about Mandy, her lodger and chocolate-making apprentice, soon to become the sole tenant of Hope Cottage when Libby moved into Max's house near the sand dunes. She didn't seem to notice that Max still stood by the open driver's door, answering in grunts, not hearing a word she said.

Stella. After all these years?

'Well, let's go,' Libby said.

'Yes, sorry.'

He made an effort to pull himself together, climbed into the car and started the engine.

'Who was it, anyway?' Libby asked.

He couldn't tell her, not now. He couldn't spoil her excitement over the wedding. 'Old colleague,' he muttered, and the lie seemed to hang in the air, like a cloud.

'One of your old business mates? Did you get cut off?'

'That's right. Might be some work coming my way. I'll call back, later.'

* * *

For once, Max wished he were anywhere in the world rather than inside Libby's cosy Hope Cottage.

They were alone, for Mandy was at Brown's Bakery, keeping the business turning over until it moved to its newer, bigger, swankier premises in Exham.

Usually, Max loved to sit at the breakfast bar, smelling Libby's cooking and guessing wildly at the ingredients of her recipes.

'Is that saffron?'

'In free cakes for the History Society? Not likely. Have you any idea how much saffron costs?'

This afternoon, Bear and Shipley looked on sadly from the doorway, knowing dogs were not allowed in this professional-grade kitchen.

Max hadn't so much as glanced at their mournful faces, this afternoon. He felt like a fraud, hiding secrets from Libby.

Just tell her, then.

He knew he should. It was no secret he had an ex-wife. He'd told Libby all about Stella, long ago, so why couldn't he find the words to explain she'd contacted him?

Somehow, he couldn't bring himself to do it. Libby looked so happy, pottering round the kitchen, spooning coffee into a cafetière, opening tins, clattering plates and cups, humming quietly with contentment.

He couldn't spoil things for her, not just now.

He made up his mind. He'd meet with Stella, see what she wanted, and then decide how to tell Libby.

A weight seemed to have lodged in his stomach. Stella must be in a bad mess, if she needed to contact Max. They hadn't spoken face-to-face for at least ten years, and their divorce had been acrimonious and painful.

He accepted a slice of apple cake – lovely, plenty of spice, though probably not saffron – and considered how best to meet Stella without telling Libby.

He turned over various scenarios in his mind. A trip to Cribb's Causeway shopping centre, just this side of Bristol, to buy new clothes for the wedding? No, Libby loved shopping there. They'd sipped Prosecco at the bar, many times, and eaten Italian food in one of the restaurants, Libby criticising the carbonara sauce as too salty. She'd insist on joining him.

Maybe he'd suggest he had a business meeting with one of his clients, needing financial advice, which wasn't unusual, and say he'd take the dogs into the woods at the Avon Gorge afterwards, to make up for cutting their beach walk short.

His phone pinged with a text message, and at almost the same moment, Libby's did the same.

They grinned at each other.

'Jinx?' Libby said, as she pulled out her phone.

She squealed.

'What's the matter? What's wrong?'

Libby's eyes scanned her phone. 'Nothing,' she gasped, waving a hand to shush him.

'Come on. Tell me.'

She raised shining eyes to his. 'It's Ali. She's coming home.'

'You're kidding. For the wedding?'

Libby's eyes sparkled. Her daughter had been in South America for over a year, working for a voluntary agency, after abruptly abandoning her university degree.

'Saving the rainforest, singlehanded,' as her older brother, Robert, described his sister's activities from his advanced age of twenty-seven.

Ali had missed Robert's wedding, so Max didn't blame him for being unsympathetic. He secretly thought Libby's daughter needed what his own mother would have called, 'a good talking-to'. Not that it was his place to offer one – he'd only met her once, just before she left the country.

'Oh.' Libby's face fell.

Now what's Ali up to?

'She can't get here until the nineteenth of December. That's almost three weeks away.' Libby's hand was at her mouth, muffling her words. 'What are we going to do? The wedding's on the fifteenth. She'll still miss it. Unless...'

'We'll see her when we get back from honeymoon.' As soon as the words were out of his mouth, Max knew he'd made a big mistake.

Libby's eyes opened wide in horror. 'But... but she's coming especially. It's only a matter of a few days. We could postpone, couldn't we? Please? I really want her there. She's my only daughter and I miss her,' she wailed.

Max could hardly bear to meet her gaze. Her excitement, her happy mood, her smiles, had all vanished. There were genuine tears in her eyes as she sniffed and wiped her nose on the back of her hand. Did Ali not realise how difficult she was being?

'I'm sorry,' Libby said. 'I'm being selfish, aren't I? We'll stick to our decision and get married as we planned. We've wasted enough time, already, wondering whether to keep our relationship confined to business. And there would be so much to reorganise...'

Max might not be too good at understanding women – after all, the marriage with Stella had ended in acrimonious divorce – but even he recognised that pleading tone, and the look in Libby's eyes. Any fool could see she was going to be broken-hearted if her daughter wasn't at the wedding.

'She can't get here any earlier?' It was a last-ditch hope.

Libby showed him the text message.

All flights booked because of Christmas.

Max raised an eyebrow. *Oh yeah?*

Silently, he counted to ten. That didn't sound like the full story. What was Ali up to? Still, his priority was Libby. He wanted her to be happy on the day they began their new life together. He gave in. 'We'll rearrange the wedding. I'm sure it's possible. Good job we didn't invite too many guests. But you have to promise, even if a dire tree emergency crops up and Ali can't get here, we'll go ahead.' He sighed. This meant another round of organisation. 'We'll have to see if we can find a date when your Robert, my son, Joe, and their wives can be there.'

Libby jumped up, flung her arms around Max's neck and hugged him tight. 'I'll talk to Angela. We're planning to meet in half an hour at the new café premises, before this evening's History Society meeting. She's a fanatical organiser and she'll help me with the planning. I suppose you won't be sorry to miss the History Society meeting?'

Max gave an exaggerated shudder. 'You know how those History Society members terrify me. Talk about formidable citizens – and if it weren't for them, we'd have had fewer incidents to investigate in Exham.'

Libby chuckled. 'I think the bad eggs have left. We were sadly depleted at the last meeting, but Angela's determined to pull in new members – preferably ones with no secrets in their past.'

'Good luck with that,' Max snorted.

'I can't wait to tell Angela about Ali's plans. She'll be so pleased – she hasn't met Ali.'

That's because your daughter doesn't bother to visit her mother.

Maybe he'd give Ali that talking-to, after all, but he'd wait until after the wedding.

2

Max had little faith in Ali's reliability. What could have kept her in South America – Brazil, in fact – for so long? It must be that boyfriend she'd travelled with. What was his name? Andy, that was it. Just Andy. The man must surely have a last name. He'd ask Libby. Presumably, Andy No-name would show up for the wedding, as well.

The two of them had just better bring a decent present.

At least Libby hadn't enquired further about Max's 'business' in Bristol. Used to his occasional disappearances on financial investigations, some of them on government business, she'd hardly batted an eyelid. Her only request, as Max prepared to leave, was that he should take the dogs. 'I feel so mean, when they're with me in the cottage and I have to keep them indoors, but if I let them into my tiny garden, they make the lawn even worse. It's full of ridges and bare patches as it is, not to mention those yellow rings.'

Max joined her at the window where she stood, surveying the forlorn winter garden.

She said, 'It's a good thing I changed my mind about selling the cottage. Who'd buy a place with a garden that looks like a ploughed field?'

Always happy to have the dogs for company, Max kissed Libby and left the cottage. He turned to wave at the door, but she was already on the phone, presumably announcing the news of the rescheduled wedding to Robert. Robert would have a word or two to say about his sister.

The weather made Max's trip up the M5 a penance. Nevertheless, he wished Bristol was further away. He dreaded meeting Stella. Whatever news she had for him, it was bound to be bad.

Thinking about his ex-wife left him depressed, balanced on a painful axis of guilt and relief. Their marriage had resulted in two great gifts; Joe, their son, now a detective inspector in the West Mercia police service, and their daughter, Debbie. The old Max had thought himself the luckiest of men, with a glamorous, if demanding, wife, two children, and a job in finance that brought in enough money to keep Stella in expensive dresses and send the children to good London schools.

In one terrible day, that whole world had collapsed, when Debbie fell from her horse and suffered a fatal head injury.

Max, devastated, had been unable to help Stella. She'd been furious with him for quarrelling with Debbie that day. 'You shouldn't have let her ride when she was upset,' Stella had insisted, over and over again, as though he hadn't blamed himself enough.

Max had buried himself deeper in work, while Stella drowned her pain in alcohol.

Their divorce had been the result.

For years, Max had believed he'd lost his son as well, for Joe had stayed with his mother, but recently, the broken bond between father and son had begun to regrow.

Wrenching his thoughts back to the present, Max pulled

together the little he knew of Stella's current life, most of it relayed by Joe. She lived in Surrey with a glamorous young entrepreneur, younger than Joe, reputed to have made millions from property development. Ivor Wrighton, that was the name. Max had exchanged an occasional, formal Christmas card with Stella over the past ten years or so, but they hadn't met. She'd seemed as reluctant as he to keep in touch.

The mere idea of seeing her in person tied his stomach in knots.

He drew up next to Leigh Woods and parked, making bets with himself over which car belonged to her. Not the Porsche. Too flashy. Stella's faults had never included ostentation.

Ah. A BMW 8 Series was parked two cars away. That was more Stella's style.

Bear and Shipley tumbled over each other in a scramble to get through the door of the Land Rover. 'Settle down, boys. Best behaviour, or I'll shut you in the car.' Max climbed out, clipping leads to the dogs' collars.

Stella, a horses and dogs country-lover, had asked to meet here, in the woods, rather than in a hotel. A little clandestine, Max thought.

Once well away from the road, he let the dogs run free, trotting behind them through the trees.

The path took a turn to the right, and there was Stella, in a clearing, waiting, peering at her watch.

Max fought an instinct to turn tail, run back to the car and speed home to Exham. Instead, he called back the dogs and forced himself to keep walking, as though into battle, Bear and Shipley positioned like a pair of body guards, one on either side of him.

'Hello,' he said.

At least Stella didn't attempt a handshake, or worse, a hug.

Slim and tall, she wore jeans and a Barbour coat, her neck muffled into a scarf. Skiers' ear warmers partially covered the hair he remembered as expensively streaked blonde, but which had now turned stylishly white. Turning fifty, Stella remained a striking woman.

'Thank you for coming,' she said, 'I didn't know who else to turn to, and I didn't want to upset Joe. But you know everything about computers and fraud, don't you?'

'I wouldn't go that far, although I still take clients. But surely you don't want to employ me?' The thought horrified him.

She twisted her gloved hands together.

She hadn't yet met his eyes. This clearly wasn't a business deal. What could be wrong?

Bear, friendly as ever, padded towards Stella. She bent down to pet him, and looked up at Max with a quizzical smile. 'Dogs, Max? You?'

Shipley, on his best behaviour, joined Bear, only some noisy panting and a lolling tongue betraying his excitement at meeting a new friend.

'It's a long story.' One Max didn't want to share. 'Tell me what you need.'

She was looking around now, expectantly.

'Are you waiting for someone?' he asked.

'Hoping not.'

That made no sense.

'I'm sorry to call you away from Exham,' Stella began, another smile flitting across her face. She had never liked the place. Exham, she'd declared, was too quiet, too dull, for her. That was before the series of murders Libby and Max had helped to solve. 'You see,' Stella said, 'someone's looking for me.'

'Looking for you? Who? Why?'

She grimaced, 'I don't know.'

This was like getting blood out of a stone, and Max's feet were cold. 'Why don't we find a pub, or something, and you can tell me all about it in comfort. Are you booked into a hotel?'

She gave a short laugh, the sound grating on his ears. 'Don't worry, I won't be appearing in Exham on Sea to spoil your small-town contented idyll with your little friend, Libby. Oh, yes, don't look so surprised. Joe's told me all about her, and the investigations you run together. That's why I'm here. I'm in Bristol for a few days and I thought you could help me. Ivor's going to join me in a couple of days, for a little holiday.'

'Ivor? Your –' what should Max call this man? He was pretty sure she wasn't married at the moment. Maybe toy boy fitted the bill best. He swallowed a grin.

'Ivor is my friend,' Stella said, with dignity. 'We share a home.'

Max sighed. 'Are you using me to make this Ivor jealous?'

Stella took his arm. 'Oh, no. I just want to consult you about something.'

A free consultation – just like Stella.

'Walk with me for a while,' she said. 'Your dogs will love it in these woods.' That was true, at least. 'It's good to see you again. You look well. I'd say retirement suits you, but Joe tells me you've been busier than ever. Fighting crime seems to run in the family.'

The edge had left her voice and Max could hear echoes of the old Stella. He'd loved her once, very much, before the marriage went sour.

They strolled through trees where the wind barely reached, reminiscing. They talked of Joe, happily married and moving fast up the police hierarchy in Hereford, and even, hesitantly, touched on Debbie's death.

For Max, the raw, unbearable agony had calmed to a lower-level ache. Now, he could remember some of the happy moments of Debbie's short life. He liked to recall her as a four-year-old, dancing round the sitting room in a ridiculous pink tutu, singing, 'Look at me, Daddy, look at me.' At school, she'd shone at maths, once winning a school prize, and he'd treasured a secret hope she'd grow up to be a scientist.

Stella cleared her throat. 'I know you blamed yourself for Debbie's death, but at least she died doing something she loved.'

Max felt a mild resurgence of affection for Stella. Maybe time really did heal, a little.

'Do you think we'd still be together, if Debbie hadn't died?' she asked.

Surprised, Max took a moment to think. Would they? Yesterday, his answer would have been an emphatic 'no.' Their marriage had collapsed under the weight of his guilt.

'I honestly don't know,' he said.

Stella laughed, suddenly, harshly, breaking the spell. 'Don't look so worried. I don't want us to get back together.'

He dropped her arm, annoyed. 'What's this problem you want to consult me about?'

'Some odd things have happened, and I thought, for old times' sake, you'd help me out. I didn't want to worry Joe.'

'If I can.' Max was cautious. The last thing he wanted was to become embroiled in Stella's life. 'What kind of odd things?'

'I'm getting phone calls with the caller number blocked, and when I answer, the line goes dead. Then, I get funny emails, too, and I don't know where they come from.'

'What sort of funny emails?'

'I had one telling me the Inland Revenue are chasing me, and another said I was owed £2000.'

'You didn't click on any of the links, did you?'

'No, I'm very careful. It's the withheld number calls that worry me – they've been coming in the night as well as during the day.'

Max felt on safer ground. Her worries were quite common.

With the internet accessible to everyone, cold-calling, scams and phishing attempts at identity theft were two a penny. Probably, Stella had simply been one of millions targeted by fraudsters. At least she had the good sense not to click on links.

'Block the calls, report the emails and change all your passwords. I don't think it's anything to worry about, but don't click on anything, or give away your bank details or passwords. It's all a try-on, but send anything that worries you to me and I'll look at it.'

'Thank you. Max. I know it's not much to go on, but I really feel as though someone's after me. For one thing, how do they know my email address?'

Max shook his head. 'It's upsetting, but it's not personal. Scammers buy lists of addresses and phone numbers. They don't know you.'

He'd worked on cyber fraud many times with his clients. As a financier-turned-investigator, he'd travelled deep into the darker side of the world wide web, and it was familiar territory.

The least he could do was try to trace the emails. 'Look, it's getting dark, and I have to get back to Exham.' He wondered how much of this incident to relate to Libby. He wanted to tell her, to be as open and honest with her as she was with him, but he dreaded pulling her into the mess of his earlier life with Stella. His instincts always told him to solve his own problems.

'Where are you staying?'

She looked surprised. 'The Avon Gorge Hotel, of course, just for a couple of nights. Then, Ivor's joining me.'

Trust Stella to find the best hotel in the area.

'Here's my email address.' He fished around in his pocket, pulled out an old business card, and handed it over. 'Send me everything strange you receive, and I'll look into it. I have your phone number and I'll get back to you as soon as I can.'

'Thank you, Max.' She turned one of her best, full-beam smiles on him – oh, how well he remembered it – and walked away. He watched until she left the trees and reached her car.

With a wave, she drove off.

Max's spirits rose as her car disappeared. He called for the dogs. 'Well, Bear, what do you think of my ex-wife?'

Bear pulled his head away from Max's hand. Max followed the direction of the dog's gaze to see Shipley, who until now had been trotting happily through the woodland, searching for rabbits and following the scent of hidden deer. The springer spaniel stood several yards away, stiff, his body trembling slightly. He barked, once.

Bear left Max's side, lumbering across to see what Shipley was up to, and whined.

'What are you doing?'

Bear had begun to scrape at a pile of oak leaves, newly fallen, not yet rotted down into compost. Max joined the dogs and took hold of Bear's collar.

Shipley ignored him, standing rigidly to attention, his eyes on the ground.

Max peered at the leaves. They lay in a heap. Had the strength of the wind thrown them together, or had they been piled up deliberately?

His heart pumping, he stirred the leaves, parting them gently with his gloved hands.

The pointed toe of a tan suede boot poked through.

Moving the leaves with even more care, Max uncovered the bottom half of a pair of coffee-coloured leggings, the second boot half on and half off. Working carefully, a lump of horror blocking his throat, he found a fur-lined jacket, and finally, gently, stroked the remaining leaves from a pale, mud-streaked face.

The middle-aged woman's dark hair was tangled with mud and debris, her eyes open, her mouth a little ajar.

Max's hands shook. He'd never been the first to find a dead body before, despite the murders he'd worked on. He straightened up, taking deep breaths, fighting to stay calm. 'Well done, Shipley,' he muttered, his voice muffled. He coughed. 'And you, too, Bear.'

He extracted dog treats from one pocket and his phone from another, handed the treats to the dogs and called the police.

Libby stood in the empty space that would be, if she had anything to do with it, Exham on Sea's favourite café. She tugged her coat closer, and shivered.

Angela Miles laughed. 'Freezing, isn't it? I've learned to wear my warmest thermals when I visit. I suppose the heating will be one of the last things to work.'

The shopfitters had packed up for the day, leaving ladders and shelving leaning against the walls. 'We should be open for business on time. It's just a couple of weeks, now. Owen's been here most of today, cracking the whip. The workmen speed up every time he appears and he's terrifyingly fierce with them. You'd never think that, would you?'

Angela, a widow for many years, and Libby's best friend in Exham, had met Owen Harris a couple of months ago. A good few years older than Angela and Libby, and undeniably stout, he'd seemed at first to be an unlikely match for the elegant Angela, but his needle-sharp business head concealed a warm and generous nature. He owned a string of restaurants and coffee houses across the country, had paid a generous price for Browns' Bakery, delighting the retirement-ready Frank, and was behind the expansion of the bakery into the new café. Recognising Angela's organisational abilities, he'd put her in charge as the manager.

Libby almost burst with excitement as she told Angela her news. 'Ali's coming home, after all...'

Angela's reception was all she could have wished. She threw her arms around Libby in a warm hug. 'At last. She's been away for such a long time.'

'But she can't get here until after the fifteenth.'

'She'll be too late for your wedding day? What a shame. Why not get here in time, if she's coming anyway?'

'Something about flights being full.' Libby tried not to notice her friend's raised eyebrows.

'Will you delay the wedding, so she can be there? I know you'd love to have her with you. What does Max think?'

'He's fine with it. He knew how disappointed I was at first, when Ali said she didn't think she'd get home at all. I don't think she realised how much I wanted her there.'

Angela smiled. 'I think your son might have given her a hint or two.'

'Do you?' Libby stopped and thought. That sounded like Robert. He'd always been the quieter of her two children, even a bit boring, but he would never let his family down. 'It's going to be a small affair, and I rang the registrar this morning. She said it's fine to move it back a week. It's just as well we weren't planning a full-scale affair, like Robert and Sarah's in Wells Cathedral.'

Angela raised an eyebrow. 'And, Max agreed without an argument? That's very understanding. You'll have to make it up to him.'

'He said that. Anyway, he's gone off again, to some work meeting. I've no idea what it's about – but, you know Max.'

Angela sighed. 'He's not exactly forthcoming about his affairs, is he?'

Secretly, Libby agreed, but she wasn't ready to confess, even to herself, that she was tiring of Max's absences. With hindsight, she almost wished he'd complained more about the change of wedding date. He was always calm, and she loved that about him, but she sometimes felt he hadn't let her fully into his world. He was self-contained. He loved a good argument, but Libby had never seen him lose his temper. That was good, wasn't it?

'Hmm.' Angela walked across to the door at the end of the room. 'Come and see the kitchen. Tell me if it's going to meet your needs.'

Libby had the feeling her friend was tactfully changing the subject, and had a moment of doubt. Had she made a mistake, putting Ali before Max?

* * *

The two friends spent an hour together, admiring the gleaming stainless steel, the extensive run of cupboards, the huge cooker and, especially, the hot water dispenser.

Libby said, 'I never dared have one of those in my kitchen at home. It's a hangover from having brought up two children, I think. If there's any dangerous implement around, they'll hurt themselves. Robert had his first penknife for his ninth birthday and immediately chopped a lump off the tip of his little finger.'

Angela ran her hands along one of the worktops. 'Look at this – it's your area for tempering chocolate. Is it what you wanted?'

'Perfect. And there's room for Mandy to work alongside me. She's going to take over most of the day-to-day baking, now she's passed her exams, and I'll oversee the chocolates. I'm hoping to split my time fifty-fifty between cooking and investigating, depending on the cases that come our way.'

'You mean, on how many more murders Somerset can provide.'

'We've had more than our fair share, it's true, but I'm not going to neglect the café. I still love baking and chocolates. My life's a weird mixture of jobs, I know, but I love it.' Libby walked along the stretch of cupboards, opening and closing doors. 'Frank's looking forward to his retirement.'

'I think his wife is more excited than he is. She'll have him at home all day.' Angela's grin held a hint of wickedness. 'Under her feet. I think she has a shock coming. He's been at the bakery from dawn to dusk all his working life, and she's used to having the house to herself. At least he won't overwhelm her with chatter. Frank only talks when he has something to say.'

'Unlike the rest of Exham on Sea and its thriving grapevine.'

Angela looked at her watch and gasped. 'Talking of which, if we don't go now, we'll be late for this evening's History Society meeting, and it's my first as chair.'

Libby held up a warning hand. 'Don't tell people about Ali or the wedding. We're trying to keep it quiet. Just family, plus you and Mandy, of course.'

'Good luck with that in Exham,' Angela chuckled. 'But they won't hear it from me.'

* * *

Libby followed her friend's car the short distance from the site of the soon-to-open café to Angela's tastefully furnished, double-fronted Georgian house on the edge of Exham on Sea, over-looking the golf course.

Slightly breathless, they switched on a kettle and transferred Libby's cake from the boot of her car to a silver Wedgwood cake stand.

Founder members Margery and William Halfstead were the first to arrive.

William greeted Angela with a resounding kiss. 'So kind of you to let us meet here.'

Margery, his wife of forty years, beamed lovingly. 'Now, William, you leave poor Angela alone.'

Angela ushered the next arrival, Annabel Pearson, into the room. Libby watched with interest. Were they in for fireworks this evening? There was history between the Halfsteads and Annabel.

Sure enough, as the newcomer sank into the comfortable, cushioned window seat built into the solid walls of the house, Margery stiffened. She'd suspected her husband of an affair with Annabel, soon after the younger woman's recent arrival in Exham. Margery had seemed blissfully unaware of the fact that William was twice Annabel's age. In any case, he had never been the most handsome or dynamic man in Somerset. Love, Libby had concluded, could indeed be blind.

At least Margery had discovered her mistake in time, and Annabel never knew she'd been the grain of sand in the oyster of the Halfsteads' newly revitalised marriage.

As the room filled with people, Libby sliced cake, passing it round to coos of delight.

'Please, please, give me the recipe,' Annabel begged.

The doctor's wife, Joanna Sheffield, interrupted. 'You won't believe what my daughter did today,' she announced,

Seven-year-old Susan, apparently top of the class at school, had starred that very morning in a presentation to parents: 'Exciting ways of recycling plastic milk bottles.'

'How nice.' Ice crackled in Annabel's voice. There was no love lost between those two women.

A double ring on the doorbell saved the society members from further examples of Susan's brilliance. Angela welcomed retired teacher, Jemima Bakewell, into the room, introducing her to the newer members as an expert on local history. She avoided mention of Jemima's role in the murder on Glastonbury Tor, as a result of which one of the teacher's old colleagues was safely incarcerated in HM Prison Exeter.

Dr Phillips, the librarian from Wells Cathedral, followed her in. 'Good evening, everyone.' He unwound several metres of scarf from around his neck, nodded vaguely around the room and settled himself beside Jemima on one of Angela's sofas, cracking his knuckles with glee at the sight of Libby's cake.

Angela picked up a tray of glasses from her marble-topped console table and called the meeting to order. 'Thank you all for coming. This evening, Dr Phillips—'

'Do call me Archie.'

Angela didn't miss a beat. 'Archie has very kindly agreed to talk to us about the history of Wells Cathedral Library.'

'Excellent idea, mulled wine,' Archie Phillips enthused, downing his drink in one gulp and waving the empty glass hopefully at his host. 'Soon be Christmas. So glad to be here,' he added. 'Must be one of the most eventful history societies in England.'

Was that shiver down Libby's spine caused by the ghost of poor, dead Beryl Nightingale, long a stalwart of the society, who'd died before delivering the talk she'd longed to deliver? Her ancestor's claim to fame as a pioneer in the post office remained uncelebrated. Libby might ask Robert, a keen student of genealogy, to do a little research on the topic. Draw up Beryl's family tree, perhaps.

While Archie Phillips distributed photocopies of illuminated pages from the oldest book in the cathedral library, Annabel said, 'Have you heard about Gladys Evans' younger sister, Carys?'

Every head swung round at the hint of gossip. A touch of pink glowed on Annabel's cheeks.

'A rumour about Carys? I've heard several,' Joanna said. 'Did you know she's on her fourth husband?'

Annabel's glare would have stopped an angry rhino in its tracks, but Joanna noticed nothing. She brushed imaginary crumbs from the front of her green jumper – Libby was almost certain it was cashmere – and went on talking. 'I've heard husband number three –they divorced some time ago – is halfway through a couple of years at Her Majesty's pleasure after breaking into a vaping shop in Weston-super-Mare. I heard she met the next man at number three's hearing in Taunton Crown Court. He was a witness in some other case.'

A stunned silence fell.

Margery Halfstead cleared her throat. 'Could I possibly have another slice of your cake, Libby dear?'

Annabel raised her voice. 'Actually, I was going to tell you about Carys Evans' poison-pen letter. Well, I say letter, but actually, it's an email. She had an email from someone she doesn't know, containing a ridiculous nursery rhyme.' She dropped her voice to a husky murmur. 'I saw Gladys at the florist shop this morning, and she told me all about it. She was copied in, I suppose to embarrass her sister.' She looked from one face to another, finally resting her gaze on Joanna. 'Shall I tell you more?'

Joanna shrugged.

Annabel raised both hands to shoulder height, flexing her fingers in the air-quotes gesture Libby especially disliked.

'Lucy Locket lost her pocket,

Kitty Fisher found it;
Not a penny was there in it,
Only ribbon round it.'

Annabel's eyes checked that everyone was listening, but she need not have worried. A pin falling would have reverberated louder in that room than a shotgun fired into the peace of Wells Cathedral.

Satisfied, Annabel finished quoting the email, with emphasis, '*Thought you'd get away with it, did you, Kitty?*'

'Good gracious me.' Angela's voice broke into the shocked silence. 'How very nasty. Does Carys know who sent it?'

'It came from one of those secret whatdoyoucallits – IPs or VPNs or something, – anyway, an address you can't track,' Annabel said.

Libby cleared her throat. 'It's the sort of address people use when they're trying to defraud you. Max will know what it's called.' She wished he were there with her. He'd love it. Computer crime was right up his street.

'We had one of those phishing letters, wanting our banking details, from an address like that,' William agreed, 'but we didn't fall for it. Called the police we did. They told us to report it to the fraud line, but nothing ever happened.'

'Government cuts, I suppose,' Margery sighed.

Libby asked, 'Does Carys understand what the email meant?'

Annabel shrugged. 'No idea. I heard Gladys mention it, when I went to get a Christmas wreath from her shop. She said her sister's devastated.'

'Eavesdropping, were you?' Joanna enquired, her voice sugar-coated.

A circle of colour appeared on Annabel's cheeks. 'I couldn't help overhearing. I thought we might be able to help. After all, this society seems to be involved in everything that happens in the area.'

'And a nursery rhyme has plenty of history associated with it.' Archie Phillips' eyes shone.

Jemima Bakewell clasped her hands together on her tweed skirt. 'That's right. You see, the rhyme refers to a pair of – well...' she blinked, rapidly, 'well, to prostitutes.'

Annabel snickered.

Dr Phillips glared. 'Quite right. Lucy Locket was a barmaid in a seventeenth-century alehouse, and barmaids were seen to be "no better than they should be". Kitty Fisher was an acquaintance of hers. The rhyme suggests she stole Lucy's pocket—'

'A kind of bag tied round her waist, under her skirt,' Jemima put in.

'Exactly. But the barmaid had no money – as compared, presumably, to the lady of pleasure, Kitty Fisher. Just a ribbon.'

Angela said, 'Well, it's an insulting email however you look at it, but it would fit better if Gladys' sister was called Lucy, or Kitty.'

Joanna said, 'I can't imagine who'd send such a thing.'

Libby watched the faces of the society members, every one animated, excited. This new mystery could help the group recover a little from Beryl's death.

Anyway, even if the society didn't follow up this intriguing puzzle, she certainly would. She was already intrigued.

4

PLOUGHMAN'S

Back at Hope Cottage, Libby found Mandy sprawled on the sofa, black hair standing in spikes round her head, Fuzzy the cat curled on her lap, fast asleep.

'I don't believe it,' Libby complained. 'She never sleeps on me.'

'You don't sit around long enough. You're always jumping up and doing things.'

'Am I?'

'It's not a criticism. We all like you for it.'

'Well, that's good.' She supposed it was a compliment, although it didn't make her sound restful, in the way Max was. Thinking of Max, she wondered if he was home. She was keen to tell him about Carys Evans' poison-pen letter.

She sometimes wondered if he found this corner of Somerset too small. He'd been used to international travel as a financial adviser, although that was less frequent these days, now most finance investigations took place online.

For now, she'd talk to Mandy, instead. 'Do you want to hear some gossip?'

Mandy dumped the cat on the sofa, adjusted the gothic, black net sleeves that matched her black fishnet tights, straightened the large Celtic cross round her neck and leaned forward, elbows on her knees. 'Course I do. You've been at the History Society again, haven't you? Always something happening there. What's new?'

Libby launched into a description of the poison-pen letter; she'd memorised every word.

Mandy grinned. 'Just when I thought life was about to get boring, what with you getting married and moving out. Now, what's that rhyme supposed to mean?'

'No one knows, really. It's a well-known nursery rhyme. Dr Phillips, the cathedral librarian, was at the meeting, as was Jemima Bakewell, and they explained its history, but it didn't take us very far, except to suggest Carys is either a thief or a prostitute.'

'Nice,' Mandy spluttered. 'Are you going to visit Carys?'

'Not yet. I'm not sure she knows she's the talk of Exham, and no one knows where she lives.'

'Come on, you can't let this go without a spot of investigating, Mrs F.' Libby loved the way Mandy spoke to her, with a friendly mix of affection and respect.

'I thought I'd start with Gladys.'

Mandy pretended to shiver. 'Rather you than me. Gladys has quite a tongue on her.'

Libby smiled. 'I think there's a good heart underneath. But, just now, I need food. Have you eaten?'

'Yes, but there's always room for more.'

Libby went into the kitchen, pulling together a supper of local Cheddar and Brie cheeses, ham and crackers, arranging it on two plates alongside a green salad, sliced apples and large dollops of roasted tomato chutney.

'Mm, a ploughman's. I'll make coffee,' Mandy approved.

Two cups of coffee later, Libby's plate was empty. 'It's late, and

I'm going to bed before I drink too much coffee and sit up twitching all night,' she announced.

Max hadn't contacted her since his trip to Bristol. She tried not to mind.

As Mandy collected the plates, yawning, Libby's phone rang. A glance at the screen told her it was Max. 'I'll take it upstairs,' she murmured to Mandy, her heart pounding like a teenager's. He still had that effect, no matter how much his absences annoyed her.

Mandy's wolf whistle followed her up the stairs.

Without stopping to say hello, Max announced, 'You'll never believe what's happened.'

'You've found a body?' she suggested, laughing.

'Exactly.'

'Don't be silly. I'm too tired for jokes. I'm on my way to bed. Where are you, anyway?'

'I'm not joking. I just arrived home after talking to the police all evening.'

Libby's laughter died. 'Are you serious?'

'Never more so.'

'Tell me more.' She couldn't keep the excitement out of her voice. 'Shall I come round?'

'Best not. It's too late, and I'm shattered.'

Deflated, Libby said nothing. Instead, she let him talk, disappointed that he didn't want her with him. If she'd found a dead body, she'd want his support.

'There's not much I can tell you, now, except that I took the dogs for a walk in Leigh Woods, and we found a woman's body buried under a pile of leaves. Shipley found it, of course. He did that pointing thing. I don't know anything about the woman, and there's no identification yet. She looked about fifty. Black hair, but with a touch of grey at the roots.'

'Cause of death?' That sounded professional. If he wasn't going to make a fuss, nor was she.

'None at the moment. I didn't get to see much – I was trying not to disturb the body, of course. I thought it looked like a blow to her head, but I'm not sure, and I didn't know any of the police officers when they arrived. They took my statement and said they'd get in touch.'

'Not a case for Forest and Ramshore, then?'

'Not so far as I can see. Come over in the morning, and we can talk.'

On the verge of agreeing, she stopped. Why hadn't he called in to Hope Cottage to see her this evening, to tell her about the body he'd found? If she'd found one, Max would have been her first port of call, no matter how late it was. 'I can't,' she said. 'I'm working at the bakery tomorrow.' She wasn't even going to tell him about Carys Evans and the email. That would serve him right.

They agreed to meet for lunch, and Libby ended the unsatisfactory call. She couldn't put her finger on it, but Max had sounded odd. Distant. If he'd been upset by finding the body, surely he would have wanted to see her straight away? Maybe he'd been more upset than he wanted to show. Had she been childish, refusing to meet him tomorrow morning?

She lay awake a long time, tossing and turning, unable to get comfortable. Something was wrong – awkward and disjointed – between Max and herself.

Was he annoyed at delaying the wedding? He was an easygoing man, avoiding fusses about arrangements, usually happy to leave what he called their 'social diary' in her hands. Perhaps she'd gone too far, expecting him to put back the wedding date at short notice. But he'd often said he was sorry Ali wouldn't be there, hadn't he?

Another thought struck. Maybe her excitement over Ali's return had upset him for a different reason. Before Libby met him, Max had lost his daughter. He didn't talk about it much, but Libby couldn't imagine any pain more devastating. Had Ali's return reminded him he'd never see Debbie again?

Libby groaned aloud. She'd been insensitive, and there was nothing she could do about it now. Tomorrow, she'd find a way to apologise. Meanwhile, determined not to spend all night awake and worrying, she opened her Kindle in search of something cheerful to read. By some miracle, the battery was fully charged and at last, soothed by P. G. Wodehouse and the adventures of Lord Emsworth's prize-winning pig, she fell into a restless sleep.

5

WAITROSE

Max had bought the large, sixteenth-century manor house, Exham House, when he retired from his job in a London bank. It now seemed ridiculously big for one person – even with two lively dogs around.

Max laid his phone down on the table in his study, wishing Libby were with him. He'd been counting the days to their wedding, when she'd move in officially. He'd reconciled himself to an influx of squishy cushions to the sitting room, and was even learning to put toilet rolls on the holder, rather than leave them on the cistern. 'Why?' he'd asked Libby. 'It's just another pointless task.'

She'd raised her eyebrows and shrugged, and he'd agreed to change. 'As long as I can keep my study the way it is.'

After hours spent poring through holiday brochures, they'd decided to take their honeymoon in the New Year. 'Somewhere hot,' Libby had said, 'but let's stay in Exham for our first Christmas together.' Max pictured the house filled with Christmas trees, decorations and cards, with the two dogs and

Fuzzy the cat all snuggled in a heap in front of a crackling log fire. He must remember to order more firewood.

Meanwhile, Bear did his best to provide company by lying across Max's feet. Shipley lay sprawled on the floor, upside down, hoping for a tummy tickle, but he'd have to wait. Max's mood, already sombre from the sight of an unknown woman in a makeshift grave, hair full of leaves, mud all over her face, sank even further as he thought about the meeting with Stella.

What did she really want with him? Was she just jealous of his new-found happiness with Libby? Maybe that was it.

There had been an odd look on her face. Stella had always set great store on the way she looked. She dressed well and he was sure she'd had a little 'work' done on her face, but today, as she described the emails, she'd looked old and tired. Dark rings had circled her eyes, her lips had thinned into a single line with her trademark red lipstick sinking into the surrounding fine creases, and her brow bore furrows no Botox could entirely erase.

What if her suspicions were right and someone was deliberately targeting her? Would the harassment escalate or would the perpetrator lose interest and move on to another victim? Until he was sure, Max had a duty to help. After all, she was the mother of his children.

He glanced at his watch. Midnight already. Would Libby be asleep? He wanted to phone again, explain about the meeting with Stella, but he couldn't bring himself to do it. Not yet. Libby had sounded distracted, almost cold, on the phone. How would she react to his meeting his ex-wife, whom he'd previously insisted was happily living on the other side of the country, with no need for any contact between them?

He should have told her before he went to Bristol, then he wouldn't be in this spot.

Maybe the best plan would be to track down whoever sent Stella the email and convince her she had nothing to worry about. Libby need never know he'd scampered off to meet his ex-wife as soon as she asked him to.

He wouldn't sleep tonight, in any case, so he might as well do something useful.

He pushed Bear off his legs, rubbing the big dog's chest as Bear grumbled, rewarded Shipley's patience with a brief tummy tickle, made a cup of coffee and settled down at his desk. The computer hummed and Bear raised his head for a few seconds before falling asleep again. He was showing his age. Max hoped he'd have a few more years in him. It would break Libby's heart if Bear fell sick – or worse.

Max checked his email. Sure enough, Stella had forwarded her mysterious messages to him.

These arrived while I was with you.

He ran through them.

I'm watching you.

The email included a photo; the back of a woman, who could easily have been Stella, shopping in Waitrose.

Don't think you've got away with it.
You'll be sorry.

Another photo of Stella, taken from the back again, at a different shop.

Max tried to be objective. Was that really Stella in the photo?

It wasn't clear enough to be sure, even after he'd magnified and enhanced it as much as possible. The photo bore all the hallmarks of an amateur attempt to frighten.

He sent Stella a quick text, asking if she recognised the branch of Waitrose as the place she normally shopped, but had no reply. She'd be fast asleep, like every sensible person at this time of night.

Max set up a photo-sharing app, and sent her the details.

If any more photos arrive, put them here.

He took a slug of coffee and forced his mind to think logically. Objectivity, that was required now. How should he proceed? The photos were unsettling. He couldn't blame Stella for being scared. Her instincts had been correct, and clearly someone wanted to frighten her. Max hoped that was all. He'd tell her to send everything to the police, but it would be difficult for them to act. Stalkers could follow their victims for many months before being caught. Stella hadn't received many emails and they'd only recently arrived. The 'stalker' might never get in touch again.

But she was right to be anxious and Max didn't like it at all.

He checked the sender's addresses. Each message appeared to come from a different country, but that was easy enough to arrange; Max used the technique himself when tracking possible criminals.

One purported to come from Russia, one from Latvia, and one from Spain. The sender knew enough about technology to hide his identity.

Using his own, untraceable IP address, Max logged onto the Tor browser, a gateway to the deeper, unregulated highways of the internet, and began a trawl through the dark web.

After three hours, he logged off, frustrated at his lack of progress. He was no farther forward, and he needed a shower to wash away the memory of some of the sites he'd visited.

6

TOAST AND MARMITE

Next morning, Libby grabbed a slice of toast and Marmite for breakfast and gulped hot tea. There was just time to dash over to Max's place before her start at the bakery, surprise him and offer the remaining half of the tea loaf she'd cooked. He'd like that for breakfast and it would show she cared.

Her purple Citroen coughed and spluttered on the short trip. Alan Jenkins, the owner of the Exham on Sea garage, had suggested she look for a new car, but she was fond of the tiny vehicle. She'd bought it fourth- or fifth-hand when she'd arrived in Exham. Alan, a classic-car lover, understood her affection for the willing little workhorse, and had nurtured it as carefully as though it were one of his precious Cadillacs, but even he thought it was time for the Citroen to retire.

Libby had also recently bought a second-hand car for the chocolate business, and Mandy used it for trips to customers and suppliers. Mandy had a knack for charming customers into making huge orders, so the investment had been worth every penny. Libby would need a different car for herself.

Of course, after the wedding, she'd have easy access to Max's

Land Rover, though maybe not the Jaguar. He wasn't keen on letting anyone drive his new pride and joy. He even spent some Sunday mornings polishing it.

Libby often borrowed the powerful 4x4 for journeys into the deepest parts of the Somerset countryside, but she was reluctant to be without her own car. It was a symbol of independence. She'd looked after herself since coming to Exham, and she wasn't going to stop now, just because her husband was a wealthy ex-banker. If she wanted a new car, she'd find the money herself. She had a few savings.

She changed gear and the car coughed again. She'd check her bank account later, see what she could afford. She didn't need anything grand.

Five minutes later, she drew up outside Max's house, admiring the graceful sweep of gravel that led to the front door. His Land Rover was parked to one side.

Her own drive at Hope Cottage was short, just enough to accommodate the Citroen. Weeds infested it during the summer and Libby spent hours digging them out with a penknife, determined not to use chemicals. The weeds would be Mandy's problem, next year, when she was the sole tenant, although Libby would always love this place, where her amazing new life had begun.

As Libby approached the door – polished oak with a heavy brass knocker – Shipley barked loudly from inside. She could hear his toenails clattering on the wood floor of the hall as she turned her key in the lock. She pushed the door open. The two dogs chased each other in excited circles, competing to get close as she pulled dog chews from her pocket and offered one to each dog.

No Max appeared, despite the noise.

As the dogs settled down, chewing happily, Libby listened.

The house was unusually quiet. Max often worked late, far into the night, sitting at his desk with a desk lamp and cup of coffee for company, but even if he'd been up late last night, the dogs must surely have woken him this morning.

It wasn't at all like Max to lounge around in bed.

She walked through to the deserted kitchen to fill a kettle and butter the tea loaf. The dogs followed behind. It was fun, allowing Bear and Shipley into the kitchen, against every rule of hygiene. She couldn't do that at Hope Cottage.

'Not long now, Bear, before we're all together, permanently,' she whispered. She tiptoed around the room, closing cupboard doors with exaggerated care. She'd give Max a surprise, make up for her grouchiness yesterday.

Bearing a loaded tray, Libby climbed the stairs to the main bedroom, as excited as a child taking breakfast to her mother on Mother's Day. She pushed the door open and stepped inside...

The room was empty.

Where was Max?

Had something happened. A heart attack or something? Of course not – but, he wasn't as young as he used to be...

Anxious, Libby ran to the en suite shower room, half expecting to find Max in a heap on the floor. It was empty. She inspected the rooms more closely. The duvet was thrown carelessly back, water had pooled on the floor of the shower, and the towels were damp. He'd slept here last night, then.

'Max,' she shouted, her voice shrill.

She sped from one room to another, opening wardrobes, calling his name. She even checked the cupboard under the stairs.

'Where is he, Bear?'

Think, she told herself. What would Max do if she went missing? He wouldn't give way to hysteria and rush around like a headless chicken.

She took a long, deep breath, aware her heart was thudding. *I'll be the one with a heart attack, if I'm not careful.*

She stroked the soft fur on Bear's head. 'He's not here, is he? He's gone out. I'm wasting my time.'

His study, that was the place to look. If he'd left any clues to his whereabouts, they'd be in there.

She drank the coffee she'd made for him, and tried to be sensible. They'd agreed to meet for lunch, so there was no earthly reason why he shouldn't have risen early and left home. He'd be back later.

But, why leave the dogs?

And, the Land Rover was on the drive.

He kept the Jaguar in the garage. She hadn't checked in there.

Leaving her empty cup beside the sink, she made her way to the garage.

Sure enough, the Jaguar had gone.

Now, Max's absence began to make sense. He'd keep the dogs out of the Jag, not wanting to spoil its pristine leather interior – nothing caused worse damage in a car than Bear's drool and Shipley's scrabbling claws.

Libby's panic turned to annoyance. Why hadn't he left her a note?

Because you'd refused to come over this morning, she remembered. She'd said she was too busy.

Well, maybe she deserved her punishment.

She trailed back into the house, wishing she'd been nicer to Max on the phone. This ought to teach her not to take him for granted. She ignored the small voice at the back of her head that whispered, *he could have sent you a text message, at least.*

Still uneasy, she returned to Max's study and settled in his chair to check for a note. There was a very 'Max' feel about the desk. Tidy, neat, with leather holders for pens, a case holding the ridiculously expensive pen Libby had given him for his birthday in October, and a pad of paper with a joke on each page. There were 365, one for every day of the year. That had been Mandy's gift.

Libby fiddled with his blotter, a barrel-shaped affair that dried ink by rolling over it. There was no note.

She shrugged. Why would there be? Max hadn't expected her to turn up unannounced.

His laptop sat on the desk. He might have an appointment in his calendar. He never minded her using his laptop, and he'd given her the password to get in, assuring her that anything related to confidential business was separately stored under different passwords.

She checked his calendar, but there was nothing unexpected there. She was about to close the machine down, when it beeped and a message flashed across the screen.

Photo from Stella.

Libby and Max used a private photo stream to send each other silly pictures, and this was clearly something similar.

She hesitated, feeling a stab of guilt at prying into his affairs, but she couldn't resist. Stella. She knew that name.

She clicked the icon that took her to the photos area, and saw an album she didn't recognise, labelled 'Stella'.

She remembered why the name sounded familiar. Stella was Max's ex-wife.

Libby swallowed. Why were they in contact? Or, at least, why hadn't Max mentioned he was sharing photos with Stella? How long had this been going on?

The stream was private. She really should turn off his computer, now, and stop prying.

But Max hadn't hidden it.

Her mouse hovered over the 'shut down' command, but she couldn't bring herself to click it. She'd come this far, snooping in his computer. She might as well go the whole hog.

She clicked again, gasped and half-rose from her seat as the picture of a glamorous woman appeared.

Libby had seen photographs of Stella, taken during their marriage. This woman was older, but unmistakably the same person.

The comment section had a remark from Stella:

Another photo.

There were two or three photos in the album, sent this morning. Libby clicked through them one by one. Photos of the woman that Libby took to be Stella. All taken from behind.

Shaking, Libby forced herself to shut down the machine, sit quietly and think.

She pulled out her phone and sent a text for Max to pick up if he wasn't driving.

I've seen the photos. Where are you? You have some explaining to do.

* * *

Max turned on to his own drive to see Libby's Citroen outside the front door.

He'd heard his phone ping a couple of minutes earlier. He parked, picked up the phone, and grimaced as he read the text.

He swore under his breath as he walked into the house and through into the study.

Libby sat at his desk, her hand on his mouse, the computer screen flickering. She glared at him.

'What are you doing here?' he asked.

'I came to see you before going to work, because you'd asked me to, and I felt mean for saying no. You weren't here, so I looked at your calendar, and the photo of your ex-wife popped up.'

He swallowed. 'I should have told you.'

'Told me what?' She rose and folded her arms, her face like thunder. It was like being a schoolboy again, in the headmaster's study, in deep trouble.

'Stella's in a fix.'

'Is she?' Libby's tone hardly sounded sympathetic. 'I thought the two of you were never in contact.'

'We weren't. I haven't spoken to her for years, but she phoned me yesterday and asked for my help.'

'So, of course, you went running.'

I can't win this argument. No point trying.

'Look, Libby. Stella's in trouble. She thinks she has a stalker. He or she's been sending her those photos, and it frightened her. That's why I went out yesterday – to find out what was wrong.'

'Hm,' Libby grunted.

He went on, 'I just popped out for a half-hour, this morning, to talk to DCI Morrison.'

'Well, you might have left a message.' Libby's face had turned quite pink.

He decided against trying to be reasonable, and kept quiet. This wasn't the moment to share the news he'd heard from the police officer.

'Well, you can be your ex-wife's knight in shining armour if you want to. Take all the time you like. I'm late for work.'

She grabbed her coat from the hook in the hall, shrugged it on, and pushed past him.

'Hey...' he tried to stop her, but she elbowed him away.

Best to admit defeat.

He said, 'Are you still on for lunch today?'

She stopped to glare at him, as if on the verge of refusing. 'Very well, but you're paying. And it's going to be an enormous bill, so brace yourself. And maybe you'll tell me what this is all about.'

She left in what Max could only describe as a flounce, and slammed the door behind her.

Libby, overdue for her shift at the bakery, found Frank loading the van for deliveries. 'I'm sorry I'm late,' she muttered. 'But it's Max's fault. I'll come in early tomorrow, help you with the baking.'

'No need. Mandy's coming. Hard worker, that one,' and Frank was gone, leaving Libby with a gloomy sense of failure and a heap of rolls to fill before the mid-morning rush began.

She'd hoped to take an hour out to visit the florist, curious to know more about Carys' email, but her pride wouldn't let her take more time off.

Should she cancel lunch with Max?

No, she wanted to know what he'd been up to with his ex-wife. She planned to get the truth out of him over the most expensive dish in the restaurant. Besides, she was curious to know where he'd been so early in the morning.

At the back of her mind, she knew she'd overreacted. She'd panicked on finding Max had innocently left his house. She'd put it down to wedding nerves, perhaps, along with a shot of guilt at delaying the wedding.

As the morning progressed, the regular stream of customers in the busy bakery gave her little time to brood. She wished Mandy were here, serving up her usual brand of common sense, along with the day's cheese and pickle sandwiches and doughnuts.

Mandy and Libby had survived some dangerous moments. Mandy had once saved Libby from a knife attack, and when Mandy's father, Bert, had threatened her mother, Libby – or more accurately, Bear – had sent him packing.

'Cheer up, Libby, it might never happen.' Alan Jenkins, the garage owner, flung open the door and burst into the bakery.

'Already has,' Libby muttered.

'That's not like you. What's Max been doing to upset you?' Max and Alan were long-time friends, ever since they'd been at school together. 'Anything I can do?'

'Thanks, but I'm being silly.'

'Not possible.' Alan was one of Libby's staunchest supporters. 'Anyway, I popped in to tell you about a nice little SUV that just came my way. It would do you beautifully, replace that purple monster you drive.'

'Can't afford it,' Libby said. 'I only just invested in the Hyundai for the business.'

'But you're not driving that one. I thought you'd like something of your own before the Citroen gives up the ghost altogether. I can do you a good price.' He mentioned a sum so ridiculously low that Libby laughed.

'You can't give it away like that.'

'Sure I can. You and Max are a couple of my best customers. You think about it, now. Call it a special reduction as a wedding present.'

At the mention of the wedding, Libby felt her lip wobble.

Alan stiffened. 'Now then. Something the matter?'

'Nothing.' Libby gulped, her voice muffled. 'Wedding nerves.' She pulled out a tissue and blew her nose.

Alan, wild-eyed, stared desperately at the door, but for once, it remained firmly shut. A lifelong bachelor, used to calling a spade a spade, he was way out of his depth with a woman in distress. He coughed. 'Oh dear,' he murmured. 'Not to worry.'

As Libby sniffed, wishing she was anywhere else on the earth than here making a fool of herself in the bakery, the door opened. Alan sighed with obvious relief as Annabel Pearson joined him at the counter.

'Everything all right?' she asked, looking from him to Libby and back, clearly curious, her eyes agleam.

Libby nodded, blinked hard and asked, 'Can I help you?'

'I came for Danish pastries. Jamie's at school, and I'm giving myself a little treat.'

As Libby served her, she said, 'I can't wait for the café to open. Angela's asked me to work part-time, waiting on tables.'

Libby tried to hide her surprise. Annabel was a widow, with an eight-year-old son at school all day. Hadn't she once said she was a trained teacher? 'You're not looking to work in a school?'

'No vacancies, at the moment. I teach languages, you see, French and Spanish mostly, but kids aren't taking languages as much as they used to. I want to get to know more people in town, and I think the café is going to be the best place for that.'

And for gossip, Libby thought. 'Good for you. You'll meet everyone.'

Alan was silent. He'd moved away, attention focused on a display of Libby's chocolates in the window. 'Could I have a box of those?' He pointed at the most expensive, lavishly decorated box of the most exotic flavours.

Libby thought she'd burst with curiosity. Who could Alan

Jenkins be buying chocolates for? Good heavens, he was blushing.

At that moment, the door burst open again, the bell jangling wildly. 'Have you heard?'

'Mandy, you're supposed to be having a day off.'

'Sorry, Mrs F, but I thought you'd want to know about Gladys Evans' sister...'

Annabel interrupted. 'Carys? The one who had that horrid email?'

Mandy glared at the interruption. 'Carys Evans is dead.'

8

FLORIST

'Carys Evans is dead?' Libby exclaimed. 'How do you know?'

'Gladys rang my mum. They've been friends for years. They still meet up every now and then.' Elaine, Mandy's mother, had moved to Bristol after her divorce from the violent Bert.

'Yes, but what happened?' Annabel interrupted.

Mandy rolled her eyes. 'I don't know many details. Just that Carys Evans' body appeared in Leigh Woods yesterday. You know, at the Avon Gorge? Mum rang me because Gladys is in a state, and she said please could someone pop round to the shop to check on her, and I thought of you, Mrs F. It's right up your street, and you're good with people in trouble.'

'Am I?' The compliment was unexpected. Libby was more accustomed to being accused of nosiness than tact. 'I don't know Gladys that well. I don't want to intrude.' Nevertheless, her mind was already racing. 'It's a bit of a coincidence, her sister dying just after that email arrived for her. Did Gladys have to identify the body?'

'Apparently not. Carys had a son, I believe. The police visited him, he dealt with the identification and rang Gladys. She says he's devastated.'

'Well, he would be,' Libby agreed. Her mind was racing. A body in Leigh Woods? Could it be the one Max had found – there couldn't be two bodies buried there, could there? And it had shown up just after the arrival of the strange email. Libby's suspicious mind was working overtime. She'd be willing to lay odds that the person Max found was Carys Evans.

Had she been murdered?

Don't jump ahead, Libby warned herself. *Not every death is a murder – even in Somerset*. Still, she was keen to check on Gladys, in any case. She'd be upset about her sister. Libby had a soft spot for the florist, despite Gladys' spiky exterior. She wasn't the most popular woman in town.

Libby hesitated. 'I should stay in the bakery, though. I was late to work this morning and I can't let Frank down any more...'

'I'll look after things here,' Mandy offered. 'I don't have any plans for today. You go ahead and visit Gladys.'

'Well, if you don't mind...'

Annabel said, 'I'll come too. Make the tea, or something.'

Libby couldn't think of a reason to refuse, although she disliked the thought of offering Annabel more gossip-fodder, and the two women left the shop. As the door swung to behind Libby, she could hear Mandy repeating every detail of her mother's call to a fascinated Alan Jenkins.

Annabel and Libby hurried down the road, to where Gladys lived above the flower shop. They threaded their way past Christmas shoppers in the High Street, under Merry Christmas banners, past shop windows bright with tinsel. Annabel said, 'Clifton Suspension Bridge is notorious for suicides, or so I've heard.'

'But anyone jumping would land way down in the gorge. Not

in Leigh Woods. Anyway, there are barriers along the bridge, now, to stop people.'

Annabel shrugged. 'If you're determined enough, there are places you can climb over the wall beside the towers. There's CCTV, though, and often the bridge keepers manage to persuade people not to jump.'

Libby shivered at the thought. She hated heights, and Clifton Suspension Bridge spanned the gorge at a dizzying altitude. Even driving across made her stomach lurch.

Annabel continued, 'I went to the visitor centre, soon after I came to Exham. It's fascinating. Did you know Isambard Kingdom Brunel designed it for a competition, but he died before it was built?' She chattered on, cheeks aglow with the winter chill and the enthusiasm of a West Country newcomer.

Libby wondered about Annabel. She'd been widowed a few years ago, and had only recently arrived in Exham, looking, she said, for a new, quieter life, where she could walk on the beach with her son and get out into the Somerset countryside. Exham, for all its quiet charm, lacked the excitement of a vibrant city like Bristol or Bath. Was she lonely? And did her young son find it dull?

None of your business, Libby told herself, as she let the recitation of facts slip over her head. Her thoughts turned, instead, to Gladys and her dead sister, Carys. Libby hadn't even known Gladys had a sister, until yesterday.

* * *

Gladys lived over her flower shop at the bottom of the High Street, next to an award-winning haberdashery, just around the corner from the site of Angela's new café. This part of town, a short stroll from the beach, felt like the heart of local Exham. It sat a little apart from the bustle of the seafront kiosks selling beach balls, buckets and spades, but close enough to the sea to attract plenty of passing trade during the visitor season.

The windows of the flower shop glittered with fairy lights, Christmas wreaths, and huge vases of dried flowers.

Annabel leaned her thumb on the doorbell, and a muffled voice from above called, 'Come in.'

The door was on the latch, so Libby pushed it open and led the way through a narrow passage behind the shop, and up a staircase.

Gladys met them at the top. A small, thin woman in her late fifties, she had a shock of wiry hair, suspiciously dark for a woman of her age, usually tamed into an untidy bun at the back of her neck. Today, her face was pale, and her hair, unconstructed, curled wildly around her face.

'Libby, it's so kind of you to come,' she said, in her lilting Welsh accent. 'Elaine told me she'd ask you to. Oh. Annabel, too.' A little frost had crept into her voice.

Libby glanced from one to the other. Another woman who disliked Annabel, as Joanna did? 'I'm so sorry to hear about Carys,' she began.

Annabel, perhaps sensing Gladys' hostility, said, 'I'll put the kettle on, if you don't mind letting me loose in your kitchen?'

Gladys made a curious gesture, half shrug and half nod, and led Libby into the flat's tiny living room; an overheated, chintzy space full of tables swathed in embroidered tablecloths. Ornaments and knick-knacks decorated every surface.

With care, Libby negotiated an occasional table dominated by a carriage clock and a porcelain statue of a boy dressed as a shepherd, and sat on a chair covered in rose-patterned linen. She handed Gladys a brown paper bag containing jam-filled pastries from the bakery – one of the florist's favourite treats.

Annabel clattered cups in the kitchen.

Gladys narrowed her eyes. 'Why did you bring her?' she hissed.

Libby, startled, stammered a little. 'She offered. She wants to help.' She leaned close and whispered, 'I think she's lonely.'

Gladys grunted. 'She's got a nose for gossip, that one. Mark my words.'

You could say the same for me, Libby thought. Rumour and hearsay lay at the heart of her methods when she was on a case. She encouraged people to talk while she listened, alert for seemingly inconsequential remarks that jolted her brain into action.

She studied Gladys, listening carefully as the florist talked.

'Down in the valley, she was,' Gladys said, her Welsh accent very evident. 'Lying under a heap of leaves.'

'Did Carys live in Bristol?'

'Not really. At least, she's been staying there recently, but she's spent most of her life in London.' Gladys' eyes slid away from Libby's face. She picked up the shepherd boy, and stroked its head.

Libby chose her words with care. 'I'm very sorry about your sister. I want to help, if I can. Max always reminds me every death is suspicious until proved otherwise. Let's face it, honestly, if someone attacked your sister, you'll want to get to the bottom of it, won't you? Maybe you have an idea or two of your own?'

Gladys nodded, but still avoided Libby's gaze.

Libby tried again. 'That nursery rhyme email was spiteful, but it may contain clues. It could tell us why someone wanted her dead.'

Gladys rose and walked to the window, watching Exham on Sea residents going about their business in the street below. 'Look at them,' she said. 'All leading happy lives, shopping and cooking, getting ready for Christmas. They're good people here. Law-abiding. Quiet. They wouldn't understand my sister, you see. Carys was a law unto herself.'

Libby joined her at the window. 'Don't you believe it. The Exham on Sea community is as full of secrets as any inner city. Look at Angela there, busy setting up the café. Her husband was killed by a rival, but she's made the best of her life and now she has a new career and a new man.' *As do I*, she could have added. 'Mandy's dad turned out to be a wife-beater, and my own husband was a selfish, weak, petty criminal. Don't be fooled by the images we hide behind or the smiles we wear, pretending all's well. Everyone has a skeleton or two in their cupboards.'

'I suppose you're right,' Gladys said.

'I won't be shocked by your sister's history, no matter what she's done. It'll be a nine-day wonder in Exham, and soon forgotten. The neighbours will be far more interested in who killed her. That email didn't seem serious at first – more like a very bad joke, but it's clear your Carys had a complicated past, and maybe that's what led to her death.'

Gladys fumbled for a handkerchief. 'You're right, of course. I'm not really surprised she's come to a bad end. I've spent most of my adult life covering up her behaviour. I should have known it would all come out one day.'

'Why don't you tell me about her?'

At that moment, just as Libby thought Gladys was about to divulge an important piece of information, Annabel returned from the kitchen, bearing a tray laden with mugs, a milk jug, a biscuit tin and a bag of sugar. 'Couldn't find the sugar bowl,' she sang out, as though dispensing refreshments at a tea party.

She could use a little tact, Libby thought.

Gladys muttered. 'Get rid of her.'

Libby thought fast. 'Annabel,' she said, 'I wonder if you'd

mind popping back to the bakery. I only brought two cakes. Could you ask Mandy for a mince pie?'

'Oh, not to worry. I'll stick to biscuits.' Annabel was either too thick-skinned to take Libby's hint, or determined to hear whatever Gladys was about to say.

Gladys said, 'Well, could you run downstairs to the shop and put together a bunch of dried flowers for me? Carys always loved my flowers. I'd like to put some on the mantelpiece, beside her photo.'

Annabel hesitated, but gave in. 'Oh. Very well.' She disappeared downstairs, clutching the bunch of keys Gladys had retrieved from a jar on the table.

'Now, then.' Gladys had bounced back a little, regaining some of her usual sparkle. 'I'll tell you about Carys.'

As she listened, Libby moved to the mantelpiece, to look at the photograph in its silver frame. She saw a younger, prettier version of her sister, with the same dark hair, blue eyes and black eyelashes, showing their Welsh ancestry.

'Carys,' Gladys said, talking fast, her glance constantly flickering to the door, as though she was keen not to let Annabel hear a word. 'Carys was my little sister. She was born when I was almost grown, and she was the centre of our family.'

Libby lifted the photo and tilted it to catch the light. 'A pretty woman.'

Gladys nodded. 'Indeed, she is. *Was*, I mean.' She sniffed, her face crumpling. She blew her nose heartily on a pocket handkerchief. 'Our Carys grew up in a bubble of admiration. Everyone loved her. She wasn't too clever at school, but then, nor was I, but she could run like the wind. She played tennis and hockey – in the first team for both, she was.'

'Where did you live?'

'Oh, not far away from here. On the other side of the River

Severn, near Cardiff. Another quiet, rural place, with a village school and a tiny shop, but it was too dull for Carys. She wanted the bright lights, the shops and pubs and clubs, and she couldn't wait to get away from home. Neither of us was clever enough to go to university. I started work at a florist's – I've always loved flowers – but Carys, she couldn't seem to settle. One job after another, it was. Shop work locally, at first, but she found the little sweet shop and newsagent in the village too dull. In the end, she got herself a job in Bath, at the department store.'

'Jumbles?' Libby put in, and Gladys nodded.

'She seemed happy enough there. Plenty of people coming in and out. That's where she met her first husband, Peter Noakes. He worked in one of those tailors, where you can hire evening clothes – you know, for weddings and... and so on.'

The phrase 'weddings and funerals' hung in the air, unspoken.

'Anyway,' Gladys wiped her nose, tucked her handkerchief back into the sleeve of her pink cardigan, and went on. 'Peter and Carys set up home in a nice little house on the outskirts of Bath. That was back in the day, when young people could get a foot on the housing ladder. I thought she'd settle down then, but within two years, she tired of Peter, and went off with an estate agent. Mike, he was called.' Gladys gave a short laugh. 'I bet you can see where this is heading. Mike lasted just a few years, and then she was off again, with husband number three.'

Libby sat down and reached into her bag. 'I hope you don't mind if I write this down, Gladys. I want to get the names right.'

'You carry on. I expect the police will want to know all about it soon, anyway. Husband number three was Alexander, and then there was Sid and John, but she'd given up bothering to marry them, by then. I suppose that's why the person who sent that nasty email likened her to a... to a... prostitute.' She reclaimed her handkerchief from her sleeve, and blew her nose again.

'Did she have children?' Libby prompted.

Gladys pursed her lips. 'One little boy, with Peter, but when Carys left, the child stayed with his dad. He was only two. That's why they've never been close.' She burst out, 'Unnatural, that's what I call it. Leaving your little one, for a man. There's not one of them worth it, and your child will never forgive you. Never.'

Libby found it hard to disagree.

'I would have looked after little Maurice, if she'd asked me to. Instead, Peter broke off all ties with her and the family, and I haven't seen the boy for years. He'll be grown up now – about thirty. One of those – what do they call them? Millennials, that's it. Same age as my daughter, Becca, up in Swansea. I thought they'd grow up together, but that wasn't to be.'

As though drained by the recitation of her sister's past, Gladys fell silent, biting a thumbnail.

Finally, she roused herself and said, 'I can give you Carys' latest address if you want?'

Libby handed over her notebook and, as Carys scribbled, asked, 'Have you been in touch with your sister recently? Was there any reason for her to be in the woods?'

Gladys frowned. 'No reason I can think of. She came to Exham last year, for a holiday. Between men, I think, for once. Maybe she was meeting someone.' She hissed the last few words quietly, as Annabel's footsteps sounded on the stairs.

Libby took back her notebook, closed it with a snap, and dropped it into her bag. She had plenty to go on.

9

CHILLI

Lunchtime with Max was approaching fast, but Libby was still dithering over what to do. She'd been out of the bakery most of the morning, and she already felt guilty for not pulling her weight in the shop recently. Most of the work had fallen on Frank's shoulders, and Mandy's.

She was longing to hear all the details of Max's discovery of the body in the woods. She was sure it must be Carys Evans' – more than one body in the woods seemed unlikely.

Nevertheless, running off to lunch and deserting the shop felt wrong.

She pulled out her phone, looked at it, hesitated, and dropped it back in her pocket. Should she cancel?

She made up her mind. Max would understand. She grabbed her phone once more and sent a text.

Spent all morning investigating Carys Evans so need to work through lunch. Was it her body you found? Tell me all about it tonight?

After a moment's thought, she added a sorry and a single x.

His reply pinged back.

Understand, posh restaurant tonight?

And three xs.

Libby's plan fell apart when she tried to persuade Mandy to leave the bakery – it was her day off, after all – but Mandy was adamant. 'I love being in the shop. I get to be first with the gossip and Steve says he only goes out with me to find out what's happening in Exham. He's busy in London at the moment, rehearsing for a concert. Something Christmassy, he tells me, with carols, although I expect they'll be some of those modern ones, not "Away in a Manger".' She giggled. 'He'll be home at the weekend and all this is my way of asking you to take over my shift on Saturday so I can be with him, and I'll finish yours here.'

'I can stay for a while. Many hands, and all that.'

Mandy rolled her eyes. 'That's just silly. I can cope. You get off and solve Carys Evans' sudden death. I can see you're dying to do some thinking. Just make sure you tell me everything. Oh, and maybe you could plan some new chocolates for Jumbles. They're screaming for more – they sell them faster than we can make them at this time of year.'

* * *

Back at Hope Cottage, Libby set to work on some new recipe ideas she'd had. She opened the cupboard where she kept ingredients, and, immediately, the scents of violets, strawberries and vanilla essence hit her nostrils. She breathed them in, loving the thought of an afternoon alone in her kitchen.

As she worked, mixing and tasting, she tried to focus on Carys' background. She'd been in Exham last year, although

Libby hadn't seen her – but maybe some of the other residents knew her.

Her hands were busy with a bowl full of pistachio-flavoured cream, but for once, mixing and blending failed to soothe Libby. A barrier seemed to have appeared, cutting her off from Max. They'd shared so much recently. Why hadn't he shared the truth about Stella? And, why had Libby herself found an excuse to cancel their lunch?

A knot had formed in her stomach. Surely she wasn't jealous.

The doorbell rang, and she caught her breath. Was that Max, coming to see her because he couldn't bear to wait until the evening?

She ran to the door, hands covered in cream, but he wasn't there.

Angela stood on the doorstep. 'I don't want to bother you if you're busy.'

Libby hid her disappointment and waved her friend into the kitchen.

'I dropped into the shop, and Mandy told me you'd come home to work. So I thought, why don't I come over and beg for a taste of whatever it is you're making?'

Angela, Libby's best friend, had been transformed since meeting Owen, and she was tireless in planning for their new venture, the café. Always elegant, she wore her grey hair in a variety of neat styles, including a chignon, whose ability to stay in place all day astonished Libby. But recently her cheeks had been pinker, her eyes brighter, and her features more animated as her brain dealt nimbly with every problem arising from the imminent opening of the café.

Libby was certain she hadn't come to aimlessly eat chocolate.

Taking a seat at the table in the corner of the kitchen, safely distant from Libby's worktop, Angela unloaded a pile of neat files from a briefcase, cunningly disguised as a tote bag, but containing rigid dividers, spaces for phones and pens, and locking compartments for sensitive documents.

Libby was seized with envy. She carried her shabby notebook around in a battered brown leather shoulder bag. 'Are we going to make plans?' She was as excited about the café as her friend.

'If you don't mind?'

'I can talk and work at the same time. Have a chocolate.'

'I thought you'd never ask.' Angela took one from the plate of misshapes Libby always kept to hand. 'Good grief, whatever's this?

'Oops. Should have warned you. That's chilli, but I overdid it.'

'I should think you did.' Angela staggered to the sink and filled a glass with water, her eyes watering. 'Do people actually like this flavour?'

'Apparently. They buy them, anyway, which suits me just fine. Did you know, the Aztecs drank chocolate flavoured with chilli?'

'No wonder they died out.' Angela wiped her eyes and sat down again. 'I'll stick with coffee creams in future. Anyway, shall we talk about the café? It seems safer.'

'Go on.' Libby added a drop of lemon essence to her mix.

'We're putting the final touches to the interior decoration. We're going for a typically English seaside feel, to work with your "Baking at the Beach" cakes and, of course, the West Country scones.'

Libby put in, 'Mandy's been working on those. Her scones are light as air these days.'

'She's had a good teacher in you. Now, we want a "beach café" feel for the décor, even though we'll be in the High Street, not on the beach. It's only a four-minute walk away; I timed it. I'm ordering a driftwood sculpture for one corner of the room. Do you think a palm tree in the opposite corner would be too much?'

'Sounds great to me.' With Angela's enthusiastic management skills, the café was practically guaranteed to be a success.

'There's one huge problem,' Angela said.

'Oh? It sounds to me as though you've got it all covered.'

Angela chuckled; a musical sound that Libby envied. 'We don't have a name yet. We keep calling it the café, or the Exham on Sea café, but I think we can do better than that. We need ideas.'

'Hm.' Libby stopped mixing, and thought. She drew a blank. 'Why don't we have a competition? People send in their suggestions, you set up a shortlist to avoid ending up with Cakey McCake Face or anything daft like that. Then you could have a draw for the winning entry. The prize can be a basket of goodies.'

Angela's grin almost split her face in two. 'You're a genius, Libby. Max is a lucky man.'

'Hm.' The knot in Libby's stomach tightened.

'Do I sense trouble?' Angela was immediately sympathetic.

Libby, suddenly relieved to talk to a friend, explained that Max's ex-wife had been in touch, and he'd rushed off to see her without telling Libby.

'And that's a problem because...?'

Libby frowned. 'Why didn't he tell me?'

Angela raised her eyes to the heavens. 'Because he didn't want to upset you.'

'That's ridiculous. I wouldn't have been upset.'

'And yet, you are...'

'A bit. It's the secrecy I can't stand. I want to share things with him, but he doesn't seem to feel the same way. He doesn't tell me things. Why does he have to keep secrets?'

Angela doodled on the top of her sheaf of papers. 'I think each of you is about to discover you carry baggage from your past histories. You're no spring chickens and you've had separate experiences that made you the people you are now. Max's life events are part of him and they include an ex-wife, the shocking, painful loss of a daughter, and a divorce. Give him time. He's crazy about you. If you're worried he's going to cheat on you, I can tell you, you're making a big mistake. Trust him.'

Libby bit her lip. 'You're right. That makes perfect sense, but it's difficult.' She watched Angela tidy her papers into a pile and centre them on the table. 'I'm going to have to work at this marriage thing.' She waved a wooden spoon at Angela. 'Now, what about you and Owen? Will you be taking the great leap into the unknown of a second marriage?'

Angela tucked her papers away in the stylish briefcase/tote. 'Too soon for that. We're happy at the moment...' Her phone trilled. 'Sorry, I need to answer. It's the shop fitter. He's called three times already, today, and he never takes any notice of anything I say, so I don't know why he bothers. He always refers back to Owen. The brotherhood of men, I suppose.'

As Angela sorted out the latest issue with progress on the café, Libby sent Max another text.

Can't wait to see you later.

The knot in her stomach had untied itself. This time, for good measure, she added a string of xs and a champagne emoji.

10

CAKE AND BISCUITS

Max's spirits had plummeted as Libby left the house that morning. Just as he feared, she'd been furious to discover he was seeing Stella. He'd handled it like an idiot, and made matters worse by taking her at her word when she said she didn't mind him seeing Stella. Of course, she did.

'Bear, I don't understand women,' he lamented. 'She said she wasn't coming over this morning, so I went out to catch DCI Morrison before he went into some meeting, and now she's mad with me for that. She even blames me because she made herself late for work.'

Bear gazed back at him with solemn brown eyes. 'Yes, you know what I mean, don't you? And there's Stella. I feel responsible for her, but I know almost nothing about the way she lives now, and I don't want to get involved in it.' Bear grunted, sympathetic to his mood. 'Maybe she could get her latest man, this Ivor person, to pay for some protection. That's what celebrities do. He's meant to be rich, after all.'

He sent a text to Stella, suggesting that, and she pinged him back with a thumbs-up sign. She wasn't too scared, then. Max could leave her to Ivor while he worked on the emails she'd received.

He sat on the floor and rubbed Bear's stomach. Shipley, never wanting to miss out on attention, galloped across and wriggled his wiry body in between Max and Bear. 'But as for you, Shipley, what are we going to do with you? You're beautifully behaved – well, most of the time – but the trainer reckons you're still too excitable to go into police work.' He rubbed the dog's droopy, furry ears. 'Never mind, we still love you.'

How calming it was to talk to dogs.

Bear scrambled to his feet, awkward, his back legs stiff.

'You're getting on, old chap,' Max said. 'Libby wants you to visit the vet, see if you have a touch of rheumatism. I could do that tomorrow – get back in her good books, maybe. Good idea?'

Neither dog seemed to have an answer, but Max rang Tanya, the local vet, and made an appointment for the next day.

He walked the dogs through the local fields, letting them off their leads, for most of the farm animals were housed safely inside for the winter. Bear, he noticed, kept close to his side, walking at a human pace, while Shipley raced backwards and forwards.

While they were out, a text arrived from Libby. She'd cancelled their lunch, but she often had to do that, if the bakery was busy. She sounded cheerful enough. They could straighten things out over dinner.

Max ate a solitary meal of a dried-up ham sandwich at home, ruminating on his early-morning conversation with DCI Morrison about Carys Evans. The police officer had been as lugubrious as ever, his moustache seeming to droop with sorrow as they talked.

'No cause of death, yet, beyond that blow on the head. No obvious weapon, but plenty of branches around. My colleague in

Bristol's handling the investigation at the moment, but there's no reason why you shouldn't look around a bit, use your local knowledge, and Libby's as well. Your usual rates?' Forest and Ramshore received a minimal payment for their services with the police.

'That's fine, unless you need more than background information. If you do, we'll have to discuss the finances a little more.'

Morrison had sighed, looking even sadder than usual. 'My poor budget...' he'd lamented.

Max had a free afternoon. The best thing to do, he told Bear and Shipley, was to sort out Stella's problems as soon as possible.

He made himself comfortable at his desk. A plateful of Libby's chocolate cake and a tin of home-made biscuits at his elbow, he began a search through every piece of information about Stella he could find.

There was very little. She seemed to belong to few online groups or forums. She had a Facebook page, but it was sparse. There were a couple of photos of Joe with his wife, Claire.

Max scrolled further and caught his breath. There was Debbie, their daughter. Max carried the same photo in his wallet, and the sight of it never failed to hit him like a punch in the chest. He moved on to a holiday picture of Stella herself, beautifully styled as always, on a cruise. There was no sign of a companion. Presumably he – Max would lay bets it was a 'he' on the cruise with Stella – had taken the photograph.

He looked through the 'friends of' section of Facebook. There was more to see here. Stella was 'friends' with sixty-four people. Max groaned. Not so many by Mandy's standards, but sifting through them would take forever.

He stopped and ate the cake. Shipley begged, pathetically, but Max remembered Libby's warnings about chocolate being poisonous for dogs and fed him dog biscuits instead. Anyway, he wanted the cake for himself.

Scrolling through page after page of names and photos, now and then, Max recognised a face. There was the woman who'd lived next door to Max's family in London, back when the children were young. Wilhelmina, that was her name. A Dutch lady, married to an Englishman, she'd spoken better English than Max himself. Temporarily diverted, he looked through her page, interested to find her two children, now married adults, and a tiny grandchild.

A twinge of envy at this evidence of family life surprised Max. He suddenly missed Libby, with a sharp pain low in his stomach. He'd lost one marriage. Whatever he did, he mustn't mess up this second chance at happiness.

At that moment, his phone pinged with another message from Libby. He sat back, phone in hand, and read it through, twice. After a long moment's thought, he sent back a cheerful, emoji-filled text and returned to his task.

Two slices of cake and several cups of coffee later, he'd made a list of ten people both he and Stella had known in the past, alongside a much longer list of the 'friends' he'd never heard of.

His stomach ached a little and his legs shook from too much coffee. He closed down the computer. He'd consign Stella's woes to the back of his mind, take a shower, dress in his best, and concentrate on Libby.

* * *

'Do you think we should bring Fuzzy over here and get her used to living somewhere new?' Libby asked. That sounded like the offer of an olive branch.

They were at Exham House, ready to leave for the restaurant. She'd kissed Max when she arrived, but they were being unusually polite with each other.

Max didn't blame her for being annoyed that he'd been emailing and texting Stella in secret. He hadn't even confessed, yet, that the trip to Bristol had been to visit his ex-wife. He was waiting for the appropriate moment.

'Don't cats find it hard to adjust to new places?' he said.

Libby's indrawn breath told him he'd said the wrong thing, again. It was getting to be a habit.

'But I'd love her to move in. You're here almost all the time, now. I bet Fuzzy misses you,' he added.

Libby smiled and Max breathed a sigh of relief.

'Let's try it. There's a warm airing cupboard upstairs, so she can retreat there if the dogs become too boisterous. Bring her over, tomorrow.'

He'd confess to meeting Stella once they were in the restaurant.

'Time to go.'

Backtracking on the original plan to visit a posh restaurant in Bristol or Bath, they'd agreed instead on a meal in a country pub. Max wasn't sure which of them had suggested it first, but he was relieved. Snooty restaurants reminded him a little too much of life in London with Stella, and that was the last thing he wanted to think about just now.

He wanted to concentrate on Libby.

He was relieved to find Libby seemed to be back to her usual, warm self.

Somerset had plenty of suitable places, and they settled on one in a nearby village, just a fifteen-minute drive away.

The temperature had dropped even further during the day and the wind was from the east, whistling through the bare branches of the trees. The Rising Sun was warm and welcoming, with a roaring fire, horse brasses, and whitewashed walls deco-rated with watercolours of local scenes, painted by amateur artists. Christmas garlands hung from the ceiling, and, to Max's relief, the Christmas carol music was turned down low.

Libby and Max ordered mineral water and Diet Coke at the bar. 'My waistline. I want to fit into my wedding dress,' Libby explained.

They settled at their favourite table and picked up the menu.

Libby coughed, and fiddled with the cutlery. 'By the way,' she said, 'I'm sorry we've had to delay the wedding. I was thoughtless.'

'I'm fine with it.' That was true, now. He could wait, if it meant so much to Libby. Anyway, he had far more to confess.

He opened his mouth to tell her, but just then the waiter, a tall, thin youth with a big smile, came to take their orders. Max wondered if Libby could hear his heart thumping. He hadn't felt so nervous since he'd been interviewed for his first job at the bank. He really couldn't care less what they ordered.

As the waiter left to organise two plates of lasagne, Max took a deep breath. It was now or never. 'Look, Libby, when I disappeared off to Bristol, I went to see Stella. She'd asked me to meet her – she thinks she has a stalker.'

'Has she? That's scary.' Libby shivered. 'Stalkers are notoriously difficult to stop. No wonder she got in touch with you. Did you give her some advice?'

Oddly deflated at the lack of reaction, Max asked, 'You're not upset?'

She swirled her Coke around in her glass. 'Why would I be? You didn't, I suppose, spend the afternoon alone together in a hotel room?'

'Well, no. But don't you mind?'

'Now, you're looking disappointed. Max Ramshore, I do believe you want to make me jealous.'

He thought about that for a moment. 'Maybe. Just a little.'

She turned laughing brown eyes on his face, and his heart filled with affection.

'I don't understand. You sounded so unhappy on the phone that I'd been in touch with her, never mind disappearing off to Bristol to see her.'

'That was because you were leaving me in the dark. I was annoyed when I found the two of you were in touch – but only because you kept it a secret. I trust you not to cheat on me, especially after all the things you've said about Stella, but she was a big part of your life for years and we can't just airbrush her out of the picture. What upset me is that you shut me out. Why didn't you tell me where you were going, instead of making up a story?' She set the glass back on the table. 'I sometimes feel as though I only know a part of you. There are whole areas of Max Ramshore I never see. That's what makes me jealous. Not your ex-wife.'

'Wow.' Max sat in silence.

'See, you're doing it now. Shutting me out. What are you thinking? Are you cross with me, or what?'

'I'm never cross with you. Well, hardly ever. I'll try to do better.'

Libby laughed. 'Well, that's all right then. Don't look so worried. I don't expect you to tell me every thought that pops into your head, heaven forbid, but it's safe for you to share things that matter – like Stella getting in touch, for example.'

A large boulder seemed to have rolled off Max's shoulders. He hadn't even known it was there, but relief made him light-headed. 'I promise to keep you in the picture in future.'

They toasted each other with their non-alcoholic drinks.

'Now, down to business. Tell me all about finding the body in the woods – was it Carys Evans? I'm guessing there wasn't another. Then, I'll tell you about my day.'

Next morning, they both slept late. Libby was first to venture into the kitchen, greeted with hysterical joy by Bear and Shipley. Max, who'd fallen asleep almost as soon as they arrived back at the house, was still snoring gently.

As Libby waited for water to boil, she took the dogs outside, into the garden. The air was clear, with the chill of late November, a hint of frost riming the grass. Bear moved slowly, awkwardly, but Shipley bounced with joy, dashing between his favourite bushes in search of traces of squirrel.

'Sorry, Shipley, I think you'll find they're all tucked up for the winter.'

She watched the excitable little dog. He'd been carefully trained, and had impressed his trainers with his heightened sense of smell and ability to follow trails, even though he remained too volatile for police work. Libby was sure there was a place for him with Forest and Ramshore, but she didn't know what that place might be. Perhaps the vet would have an idea.

She took breakfast up to Max, who'd woken and was padding

around in his dressing gown, hair standing up on his head in spikes. 'You look like Tin Tin,' Libby said.

'Sorry I fell asleep last night.'

'The moment your head touched the pillow. It's just like being an old married couple, already.' Libby tucked into her waffles and maple syrup. 'I'm planning a quick trip to the bakery. It's not one of my days. Mandy's in today, along with Annabel. She's going to be working in the new café when it opens, and she's keen to get started. Angela's planning to drop in as well.'

'So you're heading for a grand gossip session.'

'That's right. I can't wait for the café to open. It will be so much bigger than the bakery, and there'll be space for us all to sit down.'

'Not during the summer. The place will be crammed and you'll all be snowed under.'

'True, but it'll be quiet between Christmas and Easter. There'll be time for the business to get on its feet before the season begins.'

Max spooned sugar into his coffee. 'I'd come in with you, but I promised the dogs a trip to the vet.'

'Good idea. Tanya hears almost as many secrets as we do in the bakery. Now, I'll get going. It's almost time for elevenses, so people will be buying their pastries.'

* * *

As Libby expected, Brown's Bakery was buzzing.

'Mrs F,' Mandy shrieked as she entered. 'Wait 'til you hear this.'

'What's happened?' Libby squeezed near to the counter, between Angela and Joanna.

A babble of voices overwhelmed her.

She waved them down. 'Sorry, I can't hear a word you're saying.'

'There are more emails – at least three,' Mandy's voice was high-pitched with excitement. 'They all arrived last night, and they're all nursery rhymes.'

'Really?'

Joanna said, 'I had one.' Judging by the gleam in her eyes, the email had pleased rather than upset her. 'Jack and the Beanstalk. Total nonsense, of course.' An earnest young woman, she always looked as though she'd dressed in a hurry, despite her expensive haircut and well-chosen clothes. It was, Libby supposed, something to do with the pair of energetic children at home, and a busy, doctor husband. Today, her nail varnish was chipped. Joanna jerked her head towards Annabel, on the other side of the counter, who was conscientiously filling rolls with ham and tomato. 'She had one, too. The Queen of Hearts.'

'Sounds more like a compliment than a threat,' Libby smiled.

Joanna grunted.

Libby asked, 'Who had the third?'

Mandy whooped with delight. 'I did! Little Red Riding Hood. That's me.'

They were all focused on the nursery rhymes. Had they not made the link to Carys Evans' death? Libby's heartbeat, though, had quickened. There seemed to be emails everywhere – here in Exham, as well as the ones sent to Stella. Was it just some kind of internet craze, unconnected to Carys Evans, or was it something more sinister?

'I wonder who's sending them,' Mandy said.

Freddy from the estate agent's office smirked. 'Don't look at me.'

'We weren't.' Mandy's tone was withering.

Angela said, 'I looked up poison-pen letters, last night. They used to be quite common, but since the internet arrived, they've died out.'

'Too mean to shell out for a stamp, I suppose,' Freddy suggested.

Libby said, 'What about bullying online – through Twitter and – what's that thing you young people use – Snapchat? And trolling?'

Freddy made a show of rolling his eyes. 'You're out of date, Mrs Forest. It's all YouTube and TicToc now. No one under forty sends emails any longer.'

Frank, the baker, had been standing in the doorway to the back kitchen. He made his only contribution to the debate, 'Whatever next,' and disappeared to pull pastries from the oven.

Angela said, 'Does that mean our rhymer is someone older? Even texting feels awkward for my generation.'

Freddy snorted. 'You need flexible thumbs. Maybe they seize up in old age.'

'Don't be so rude.' Mandy was always fierce in her defence of Libby and Steve's aunt, Angela.

Just as the debate seemed about to get out of hand, Gladys pushed the door open. 'Oh, my goodness. There's hardly room to swing a cat in here, today. What are you all talking about?'

Her eyes were pink, with dark circles underneath, but she'd made an effort, applying mascara and a dash of lipstick.

The babble in the room fell away. Libby could almost hear brains whirring, as people wondered silently whether Carys Evans' death and the emails were linked. No one was laughing, now.

In the awkward silence, Mandy said, 'Your usual pastries?' while Annabel slid filled rolls into a bag and passed them across to Freddy. He edged towards the door, elbowed it open and made his escape.

Joanna looked at Gladys and confronted the elephant in the room. 'Did you know more of us have had emails?'

Gladys shook her head. 'Copycats, I suppose. Whoever's sending them should be ashamed of themselves, making fun of my poor sister's death.' Her eyes filled with tears, but she lifted her chin. 'And I'll have an extra sausage roll, today, please. I can't seem to find the energy to cook lunch.'

Angela said, 'I don't want to speak out of turn, but since Libby's here, and we all know she's an ace private investigator, why don't we ask her to find out who's bombarding us all with these emails?'

Annabel opened her mouth to speak, but Angela raised her voice.

'I haven't had one yet, but I bet it's only a matter of time. If someone in town's trying to frighten us, or if they're just playing nasty tricks, we should stop them.'

'Good idea,' Gladys enthused. 'Go on, Libby. Sort it out for us.'

12

Shipley seemed about to explode with excitement. The vet's surgery was carefully divided into dog areas and 'other' spaces for smaller, less boisterous animals in baskets and cages. This morning, the place was full of the dogs Max knew from his walks on the beach.

Despite the constant stream of treats Max pulled from his pocket, Shipley couldn't – or wouldn't – sit still. He paced back and forth, as far as the lead would allow, sniffing the floor and whining. Too many different smells, Max supposed. To a dog with such a sensitive nose, the overwhelm must be as bad as spending an hour in Exham's tiny, pier-end casino, full of flashing lights and raucous noise.

Bear set a wonderful example. He lay down, huge and benevolent, his head on his paws, and watched Shipley's antics through bored eyes. A small boy approached, standing a little way away, fascinated.

Max said, 'You can stroke him, if you like. He loves people.'

The boy stretched out a tentative hand to touch Bear's head

and, rewarded by a satisfied grunt, ran his fingers over Bear's ruff of soft fur.

'Is one of these dogs yours?' Max asked.

The boy – around seven years old, Max guessed – shook his head and pointed to a woman who sat nearby, shrugged into a bulky parka, clutching a cage on her knees. 'My gerbil's having babies,' the boy whispered. 'Mum says we have to give them away.'

Shipley, intrigued, came closer to investigate the boy. Max blocked his progress. Shipley's bouncing would frighten this shy child.

Thwarted, Shipley turned to look at the cage on the mother's lap and stood still, rigid, in his 'pointer' stance.

'My dog's fascinated by your gerbil,' Max said.

The woman set the cage down on the seat next to her, but Shipley didn't move.

The boy said, 'He's not going to eat her is he?'

Max looked into the worried face. 'Absolutely, not.'

'Mum,' the boy called. 'Can we have a dog?'

'No.' His mother shifted in her seat. 'I have enough trouble with you and your sisters, and these blessed gerbils. I should have listened to your dad. He said I was storing up trouble for myself, letting you have them in the first place, and he was right.'

Max called Shipley away. After a moment, he came and sat on the floor at Max's feet.

Before Max could talk further with the boy, Tanya, the vet, waved for him to bring the dogs into her consulting room. 'What can I do for you?' she asked.

Max pointed to Bear. 'We think he may have rheumatism, and he seems to be going deaf.'

Tanya watched as Bear walked inside. 'I'll syringe his ears, I bet that's the problem. Rheumatism may be more difficult. He looks as though that off hind leg is causing the trouble. Look, he's resting it.'

They lifted Bear onto the examination table and Tanya gently manipulated his leg. He lay still, only a sharp grunt indicating pain.

'You're such a darling,' Tanya cooed. 'Some dogs get snappy when I touch the bit that hurts, but you're just a gentle giant.' She looked up at Max. 'The most likely problem is osteoarthritis. Just like in people, it can affect dogs as they get older, and Bear must be getting on for thirteen or fourteen?'

'Something like that. Mrs Thomson – his owner – never told me his age...'

'And she died suddenly, didn't she? Not uncommon around here.' Tanya washed her hands. 'The nurse can take some X-rays – we have a machine just across the hall – and we'll be able to see. First, I'll take some blood and we can send it off to the labs, make sure it's not something more serious, such as rheumatoid arthritis, but I doubt that. That's a long-term disease that's far more common in younger dogs.'

Bear grunted again.

'Sorry, Bear, didn't mean to be rude. Honestly, Max, you'd think he understood every word I say.'

'Libby would agree. She's convinced he's super-intelligent. But don't say it too loud – Shipley gets jealous.'

Tanya opened the door and called for the nurse. 'Laura, can you do an X-ray?'

Laura had scarlet streaks in her black hair and holes in her nose, presumably for face jewellery. She avoided his eyes.

'We haven't met,' Max said.

'I just started work here, a month ago.' Her mouth turned down at the corners.

'You don't happen to know Mandy, do you? She's – er – about your age?' He'd just stopped himself calling her a Goth.

She looked him in the eye for the first time. 'We go to the same club. We met in the bakery the first week I arrived in Exham, and she took me along.'

Max smiled at the young girl. Maybe Exham would turn into a magnet for Goths in the way Brighton had for skinheads in Max's youth. Without the fights on Saturdays, perhaps. More Goths would make some of the older residents wake up.

While they waited, Tanya weighed and measured Shipley and took a good look in his mouth, ears and eyes. 'The picture of health, Shipley, and aren't you turning into a well-behaved creature. That obedience training's made quite a difference.'

'Shipley's intelligence is different from Bear's,' Max said. 'When he's following a scent, he's like a changed animal. I wish we could find a way for him to use it. At the moment, it's more of a nuisance. In the waiting room, he latched on to a gerbil belonging to a very polite little boy.'

Max described the child and his mother.

'Oh, that's Mary Atkins and Joseph. At least, I think that's Joseph. She has a proper brood of children, that one. Three girls and two boys.'

Shipley, who'd clearly had enough of sitting or standing quietly, jumped up and whined at the door as Bear arrived back with Laura.

The two women flipped the X-ray up on a translucent screen with a light behind it. 'Look – there it is.' Tanya pointed to an area of bone. 'It's as I suspected – osteoarthritis. I'll prescribe some daily medication and we'll see how he goes.'

'Don't tell me he'll need a new joint...'

'It's possible, but the damage isn't that bad, so far. We should be able to make him comfortable with tablets.'

With a smile, Laura left the room.

Tanya tidied away the X-ray in a file. 'You've cheered Laura up, anyway. She's been as miserable as sin since she arrived here. She's great with our animal clients, but less so with the humans, unfortunately, but I'm glad to hear she's made friends with Mandy. She couldn't have a better role model. Maybe she'll stay here, after all.'

And yet, not so long ago, Mandy had been labelled a bolshy teenager. 'I guess the Goth thing puts people off a little.'

'Small minds, some folk. Now, keep Bear warm. This cold weather's no good for joints, no good at all, but he still needs some exercise, especially when the tablets relieve the pain. Dogs that are bred to work – and Carpathian sheepdogs like Bear can herd sheep over miles in the hills of Romania – decline fast if they're kept indoors.'

Max rubbed his chin. 'Not sure how to reconcile both those things. Maybe he needs a treadmill in the garage.'

'Regular short walks. That's the answer. Take your cue from Bear. If he's reluctant, don't force him. You may need to exercise these two separately. Shipley needs to work off all his energy.'

'You're telling me.'

'Now, let's deal with Bear's ears.'

Ten minutes later, they left the surgery, Bear looking alert, and swinging round at every sound. Mrs Atkins and Joseph were nowhere to be seen; they were probably in with Laura.

Max patted both dogs, and congratulated Shipley. 'Not bad behaviour at all, Ships. You're learning fast.'

* * *

Later that day, Max listened as Libby described the emails with their nursery rhymes. 'We're in a brave new world,' she said, 'with poison emails instead of letters, and Facebook friends that aren't really friends, or even acquaintances. There's plenty there for us to get our investigative teeth into, so let's make a plan.'

Max tapped his fingers on the table, beating out a rhythm as he pondered. 'I've been reviewing all Stella's online friends. I suspect that, as the stalking's been online, it's probably someone she's been in touch with, even if she doesn't know them. I've asked her to go through the list and decide who she trusts, who she knows personally, and who's managed to get on the list through mutual friends.'

Libby nodded. 'The Exham emails are different, because of the rhymes. *"Lucy Locket lost her pocket."* Do you know it?'

'I vaguely remember hearing it, but no idea what it means.'

Libby explained the reference to prostitution.

Max chuckled. 'So, poor Carys had a reputation for enjoying men.'

'And discarding them at regular intervals. That makes for a useful list of people to investigate, so we can eliminate them.'

'We should take your findings to the police. There's no proof yet that Carys was murdered, although burying the body is powerful circumstantial evidence. DCI Morrison and his team aren't the lead investigators at the moment, but in light of the rash of similar online activity in Exham, and Carys' Exham connection, that may change. I suspect Morrison is already pulling strings, and the Bristol teams are always hectically busy.'

'Let's hope so. Gemma Humberstone would do a great job of researching the backgrounds of Carys' men friends.' Detective Constable Humberstone had worked with Libby on the recent murder at Dunster Castle, and after a shaky start, they'd enjoyed their collaboration.

'They're going to need a full team. Morrison's already mentioned he might call us in,' Max said.

'There's one big worry we haven't mentioned.'

'There is. The fact that Carys received an anonymous, unpleasant email before she died. It's hard to believe those two events are unconnected.'

'And in Exham, three more people have also opened rhyming emails. Mandy, Annabel Pearson, and Joanna Sheffield. I don't think you've met those two, Max. They both arrived in Exham in the past six months.'

'Isn't Annabel Pearson one of the volunteers at Dunster Castle?'

'That's right. She seems to have got on the wrong side of one or two locals.'

'Just because she's new in town?'

'Not only that, she's also an attractive widow of about forty.'

'Ah.' Max laughed. 'A femme fatale. That explains it. Some of the wives in town might well see her as a threat. What about Joanna Sheffield?'

'Hard to know her. She's about the same age as Annabel, and the two of them seem to be in some kind of competition with each other, although I don't know why. Joanna talks constantly about her two children.'

'Well, we have plenty to get our teeth into.'

Libby said, 'I thought I'd start with Joanna Sheffield. Go and see her tomorrow?'

'Good idea. Try not to frighten her, but make sure she's taking care. Anyone with an email could be in danger.'

Libby was silent.

'What's wrong?'

'We haven't mentioned Mandy. She had an email, too. Little Red Riding Hood.'

'Then, we'll have to take special care of her. Knowing Mandy, she'll already have put two and two together.'

Libby said, 'I don't like this at all. It feels as though someone's threatening the town. None of us is going to feel safe until we get to the bottom of this.'

Max's phone buzzed. 'That new constable at the police station,' he told Libby. 'Passing on a message from DCI Morrison. He wants us at the station tomorrow morning, officially, for a team meeting at nine. It's time for Forest and Ramshore to leap into action again, as civilian investigators.'

Max and Libby rose early next morning. A frost had hardened the ground, but the sun shone brightly in a pale blue sky.

Max took Shipley for an energetic run through the lanes and fields, while Libby undertook a more sedate stroll around Max's two acres of land, with Bear. He'd had his first dose of medicine last night, and seemed keen to wander along at Libby's side. 'We'll take it slowly,' she told him. 'Leave the rabbits for Shipley.'

By ten to nine, Max and Libby were at the police station, crammed into a tiny room with DCI Morrison's team, drinking watery coffee from an array of mugs and gossiping cheerfully while they waited for the boss to arrive.

Gemma greeted Libby with a grin and a hug, as though Libby was a favourite aunt. 'You did bring cake, didn't you?'

Libby pulled the tin from her bag. 'I wouldn't dare arrive empty-handed.'

'This,' Gemma introduced a tall, thin uniformed youth with large, black-rimmed spectacles and a worried expression, 'is Timothy Green, our newest constable.'

'C-call me Tim,' the young man said, with a hint of a stutter.

Libby wondered how old he was. Such a cliché, that policemen were getting younger, but this one looked as though he should still be at school.

'Pleased to meet you, Tim,' she said.

The constable's Adam's apple rose and fell in a stringy neck as he shook hands with Libby and Max. 'I've heard all about you two,' he said, with a nervous smile that came slowly and disappeared in a flash.

Libby hoped he had more confidence than appearances suggested. If not, he'd suffer in the rough and tumble of Morrison's team of energetic officers. Had he even been part of a murder investigation before this one?

The room had filled quickly with people both Max and Libby had met before. She enjoyed their banter, pleased to find they'd accepted Max and herself as part of their team. It hadn't been so easy last time, when PC Ian Smith had set out to undermine them. Smith was still in the team, relegated to note-taking, and sitting as far away from Libby as possible.

The chatter faded as DCI Morrison arrived. As ever, his face wore the hangdog expression of a man bearing the cares of the world on his shoulders. Libby happened to know his wife was a cheerful soul who worked as a teaching assistant at Exham Infants and loved nothing more than an excuse for a party.

She concentrated on the DCI's take on events.

'You'll all know by now that Carys Evans died at the Avon Gorge. In Leigh Woods, to be exact. It's outside our area, but the Bristol chaps have asked us to help them out. Very busy over there, apparently.'

He said this with a straight face. Libby could only imagine the strings he'd had to pull with senior officers to get the murder case moved onto his patch.

'The forensic examiner's report, of which you should have

copies...' He hooked a pair of narrow reading glasses on his ears, waved the report in the air and looked around, over the top of the spectacles. Satisfied by the answering nods, he went on, 'Good, then you'll see that she died from a blow on the back of her head. Swift and deadly, and unlikely to be accidental, as an attempt had been made to cover her body with leaves. That part of the woods is a little off the beaten track, and Ms Evans' body was discovered, coincidentally, by Max Ramshore, here, while walking his dogs. You all know Max, I think.' Morrison gestured towards Max. 'We don't have DS – now DI Joe Ramshore – with us, as he's gone on to greater things in Hereford, but it's good to have a member of his family as a stand-in.' That was as close to a joke Libby had ever heard from DCI Morrison, and a couple of young officers laughed, awkwardly.

'Be that as it may,' Morrison continued, 'there's a little confusion about time of death. The weather, you see. Cold. Frozen bodies, according to this chap Hamilton in his report, take longer to show rigor mortis, and once it's arrived, it hangs around far longer.' He made the early process of decay sound like a visitor who won't go home. 'The upshot is, Ms Evans probably died a couple of days before her remains were found. But that raises an even more interesting possibility.'

He paused.

Libby calculated aloud. 'The nursery rhyme email arrived on November the twenty-fifth, and the body was found on the twenty-sixth. But, counting back two days...'

Gemma Humberstone chimed in, 'The email arrived after she was already dead.'

'Full marks,' Morrison said. 'Does that mean the two events are unconnected? Or is the email a clumsy attempt to disguise the time of death? Or is there another reason?'

Max and Libby exchanged a puzzled look. What was the point of sending a threatening email after the victim was already dead?

Libby ran through other possibilities in her head. Gladys had been copied in to the email. Whoever sent it had wanted her to know – what? Was it a threat to Gladys? And if so, why not send a rhyme directly to her?

Libby's sinking feeling told her this business did not end here. As she'd suspected, everyone who'd received an email must be under threat.

As she puzzled, Morrison introduced a female Scenes of Crime Officer, on secondment from Bristol, who described various items found at the crime scene. 'Including the branch of an oak tree bearing traces of Ms Evans' blood, there are various pieces of cloth and other materials, but given the public nature of the location, they may not take us much further forward. No fingerprints were found on the branch. The assailant was bound to be wearing gloves, given the weather. No signs of a struggle, no skin under Ms Evans' fingernails, or anything useful of that sort.'

'In short,' DCI Morrison sighed, his jowls drooping sadly, 'we're going to need plenty of straightforward investigation into Ms Evans, her contacts, ex-husbands and boyfriends, sightings in the area during the previous week, and so on. You all know the drill. There are, by the way, some very unusual aspects to this case, and we have something of a head start with these. Our civilian officer, Libby Forest here, has already begun her discussions with the local residents of Exham on Sea, using her network of contacts. All of whom, I gather, meet almost daily in the, er, bakery. This includes the victim's sister, one Gladys Evans. She keeps the florist shop.'

Libby, thrust into the limelight, described the email received by Carys Evans.

Tim, the new PC, gazed at her open-mouthed. Definitely, this was his first murder case.

'And that's not all,' Libby said. 'There are three more emails – all nursery rhymes – that have dropped into the inboxes of Exham on Sea people.'

One of the admin assistants distributed hastily photocopied lists of the other residents and the nursery rhymes they'd received.

'Three more emails? All nursery rhymes? Someone's playing games,' Morrison said. His team sat straighter, almost licking their lips in appreciation of such an intriguing development. 'We need to consider whether these rhymes are coincidences, or bad jokes, or is Ms Evans' killer planning further atrocities? There are more than enough angles to keep us all busy, including taking safeguarding measures for those who've received these unpleasant communications.' He distributed tasks to the officers in the room and brought the meeting to a close.

* * *

'The problem is,' Libby said to Max as they drove away, 'we have so little to go on. The emails are shocking, but they're not threatening. They don't give us much in the way of clues. They're just everyday nursery rhymes.'

'But,' he pointed out, 'in each case, the rhyme is fitted to the recipient. Are there any other common angles?'

'Well, all the recipients are women.'

'So far.'

'Absolutely. Does that suggest the sender is a man?'

Max slowed down to take a tight bend. 'Too early to say, I would think. Received wisdom in the past was that women were more likely than men to send poison-pen letters. But that may not hold true now with the internet.'

'Modern technology makes an email much more difficult to track down than a proper letter. No special typewriter to identify, with one letter at a distinctive angle; no licking of envelopes to provide DNA evidence; no fingerprints; no way of knowing which part of the world the sender's IP address comes from. If I've got the right expression.' She looked enquiringly at Max.

'More or less, and you're right. It's all anonymous. Let's see what turns up when we talk to the recipients.'

'Can you drop me at Hope Cottage?' Libby asked. 'I've got a few phone calls to make about this change of date. Angela offered to help, which is great, as she's the best organiser in the world, but I still need to sort out a few things. A venue for the reception, for one, and the flowers from Gladys. It's going to be hectic.'

Max rested a hand on Libby's knee. 'And it will all be worth it, in the end.'

* * *

Mandy was in Hope Cottage when Libby arrived, for Annabel had taken on the day's shift at the bakery. Libby wanted to make sure her lodger was taking the nursery rhymes seriously.

Her phone glued to her ear, Mandy was conducting delicate deals with one of the outlets supplied by Mrs Forest's Chocolates.

She concluded her business, ended the call and beamed, triumphantly. 'Mrs F, I wasn't expecting you. I was chasing up a lead for the last of our Christmas chocs, and they're all gone, now. Snowmen, Christmas trees and stockings for that place in Wells. You know, on the corner, where all the Cathedral School pupils fill up on junk at lunchtime.'

'That's wonderful. You're a terrific saleswoman.' Libby said.

She smiled into Mandy's beaming face. 'But, I came to talk about your email.'

'Little Red Riding Hood? I quite like that. My black cloak has a scarlet lining.'

'So it does. And that means whoever sent the email must know you. Or, at least, they've seen you around. Maybe at the Goth club?' Libby paused. 'Mandy, I don't want to frighten you, but I'm worried that the person writing these things might have killed Carys.'

'Nah. It's just a bit of fun. Someone's having a laugh.'

'What about Carys? Her death's not funny.'

Mandy winced. 'I know. I didn't mean to sound unsympathetic, but don't you think that's just a coincidence? No one's going to bump off another three people, all in one go, are they? At least, if they are, why warn us all? Doesn't make sense. I bet the rhymes are nothing to do with that murder.'

Mandy seemed determined not to take the email seriously.

'I hope you're right, but I want you to be careful.'

'They're just a joke, if you ask me. Look at the rhymes. Mrs Sheffield's is Jack and the Beanstalk. Appropriate, no?'

'How do you mean? Oh,' light dawned. 'She's tall—'

'Like a beanstalk. Funny, really, although I bet she doesn't think so. Takes herself a bit too seriously, if you ask me.'

'What about Annabel Pearson?'

Mandy was still chattering. 'Queen of Hearts. That's Mrs Pearson. You should have seen her the other day, flirting with Freddy from the estate agents. She had him convinced she was about to buy that empty house near Max's. As if she has that kind of money – but she led him right up the garden path, like. He was practically drooling over her, and she must be twenty years older than him.'

'I'm starting to feel disappointed that I haven't had one of these, myself.' Libby said. Was she taking them too seriously? No, it all felt wrong. The emails arrived just as Carys Evans died, and Libby distrusted coincidences. 'I just hope you're right, but I'm not convinced. Keep your eyes open, won't you? Make sure there's always someone in the bakery with you, and get Frank to take you out to the car at night, now it gets dark so early.'

Mandy burst out laughing. 'Honestly, Mrs F, you're letting your imagination run away with you. I can't have a bodyguard with me all the time. Anyway, Steve will be here tomorrow, for the weekend.' Mandy's cheeks glowed. Her feelings for her boyfriend were as strong as ever. Perhaps Angela's hope that the two would eventually get married, so that Mandy would become her niece, would come true. 'Now,' Mandy said. 'Tell me all about the latest plans for your wedding. Honestly, if you postpone it any more, we'll have to kidnap you and Max and drag you both to the register office with hoods over your heads.'

Libby managed a chuckle and tried to concentrate on the wedding arrangements, listening to Mandy's description of her dress, and her guesses about Libby's own. Her mind, though, was elsewhere. Someone in Exham was playing games. Were the games entirely innocent, if silly, or was Carys' killer, like a cat, toying with its prey before pouncing? Libby shivered. What message could the Rhymer be sending? And how did the threatening email to Stella fit in?

14

SANTA SPECIAL THURSDAY

Bright and early on Thursday morning, Libby arrived, breathless, on the platform at Minehead Station, the dogs by her side. Brightly coloured bunting hung from the station buildings, and a small Christmas tree leaned at an ungainly angle close to the waiting room. A huge banner proclaimed 'Santa Steam Special', complete with a picture of a beaming, jolly fat man in a red Santa costume. A similar banner decorated the side of a West Somerset Railway steam train.

An east wind gusted across the platform, and for a moment Libby wished she had a Santa costume of her own to help keep out the chill. She hadn't expected to join a train load of children on a trip to see Santa, but when she'd called Joanna yesterday, the poor woman had sounded so harassed that Libby was happy to agree to join the train and talk about the nursery rhyme emails as they travelled.

She picked her way down the platform, through crowds of tiny, excited children wearing party hats, mothers with babes in arms, and a sprinkling of older children trying to look cool and grown-up.

The giant train let out a puff of steam, to shrieks of delight.

There was Joanna Sheffield, waving from a little further along the platform. Libby joined her.

'You made it in time. Welcome to the Santa Special,' Joanna said. 'These are my two.' She held the hand of a small girl wearing a bright red waterproof that covered her from head to toe, with a helmet-shaped peak to the hood. All Libby could see of the child was a button nose, a few strands of strawberry-blonde hair, and a pair of round blue eyes. 'This is Isobel. She's almost four, and that one' – she indicated a taller boy standing a little apart, a glum expression on his face – 'that's Jeremy. Named after my husband.'

The boy, who appeared to be about six or seven, had a shock of curly black hair falling over his eyes, and a blue anorak. 'I'm Jay,' he rebuked his mother.

'Yes, dear.'

The children were far more interested in the dogs than in Libby. Jay took up a stance beside Shipley, his attitude suggesting no one else would be allowed near. Isobel approached Bear nervously, one hand outstretched, the other gripping on to her mother's coat. As Bear pushed his head against her hand, she giggled and kissed the top of his head.

Joanna said, 'I'm sorry I couldn't talk to you at home, today. This is the annual Christmas outing for the Children's Centre at the school I work for, and it's all hands on deck to keep order. Ninety families, would you believe? It'll be a bit of a crush on the train, but we had a couple of families cancel because of the flu, and since you've had a criminal records check, it's OK for you to come along. You can help keep an eye on them all.' Libby sometimes held biscuit-decorating sessions for children at local fetes and fairs and carried out occasional cooking lessons in schools, so she felt – almost – ready to cope with anything the children could throw at her. Joanna went on, 'There's just enough space for you. And the dogs.'

'They're both well-trained. Even Shipley's learned to keep still when he's told – a few months ago, I wouldn't have dared bring him near so many children.'

'I'm really pleased they're here. My son – he has a mind of his own, as I expect you've noticed – decided this morning he didn't want to come with all the little ones, after he'd been talking about it for weeks. Kids. I don't know. Such a handful!'

Both Isobel and Jay seemed perfectly well-behaved, especially compared to a nearby family of three under-fives, already setting up a chorus of wails and demands for ice-cream and chocolate. Had Libby made a mistake coming today? How could she learn anything from Joanna amid all this bustle? But, she was curious about Joanna, and keen to find out more about her. Of all the recent arrivals in Exham, she felt she knew least about the Sheffields.

Just then, the engine silenced the crowd with a cloud of noisy steam and blew a sustained blast on its horn. The parents and children climbed aboard and settled down, clustered around the tables in the carriages.

Joanna, with the dexterity of an experienced teaching assistant, passed out crayons and sheaves of colouring paper to the children in her section of the train, and a colleague provided paper cups of hot chocolate and mince pies. 'There'll be entertainment in the carriages on the way,' she confided.

Sure enough, a team of Santa's helpers in elf costumes arrived and set up a cheerful sing-song.

Joanna remarked, 'You'll be heartily sick of "The Wheels on the Bus" by the end of the day.'

She found a seat for Libby and herself within sight of her charges, in a small oasis of peace.

'Now, you want to know about that email I received.'

Libby sipped hot chocolate.

'Jeremy says it's just envy. He says people in small southern towns are unfriendly and they don't like incomers. Not that we've come far. I grew up in Bath, and I love Somerset, but Jeremy's from Birmingham.'

Libby said, 'It just takes a while for people to get to know you, here. There are plenty of new families arriving all the time. There's Annabel Pearson, for one. She came at about the same time as you did.'

Joanna grimaced. 'I'm sure we'll find our feet, soon.' She sounded dismissive. 'It's easy for Annabel. Queen of Hearts, indeed. The Merry Widow, I call her. Haven't you seen the way all the men look at her?'

Libby returned to the email. 'As I explained when I rang, the police have asked me to talk to the recipients of the poison-pen emails. Do you have any idea who might have sent yours? It may not be anyone in Exham.'

Joanna shrugged. 'I don't have any enemies, if that's what you mean. I hardly know anyone. My family take up all my time, you see. Jeremy – my husband – works such long hours. I don't really get out much, except with the children – and the History Society, of course.'

Not much of a life, Libby thought, for a still-young woman like Joanna. When Libby's children were at school, she'd made dozens of friendships with other parents. Joanna seemed to have very few friends.

'My husband says the person sending the emails is probably a sad little man who can't get a girlfriend. There's a name for them, apparently.' She frowned. 'Incels. That's the word. Overgrown boys who spend all day in darkened rooms, playing video games and hating women. My husband says we should just be sorry for them. He thinks the person who killed Carys Evans has nothing to do with the nursery rhymes. He says it's some old boyfriend she quarrelled with. Frankly, though, the whole thing gives me the shivers.'

Did Joanna have any real opinions of her own, or did they all come from her husband?

Before Libby could delve further, their conversation was interrupted. Until now, Shipley had been content to move from one child to another, tail wagging furiously, but otherwise behaving as calmly as Bear. Libby had almost forgotten the dogs were there when Shipley opened his mouth and drowned out the noise in the carriage with a single, echoing yelp.

Libby jumped to her feet, expecting to see chaos, afraid Shipley might have frightened a child. 'What's wrong?'

Shipley, tail stretched rigid, stood immobile in the centre of the aisle between the seats, pointing his nose at a woman sitting nearby, a sleeping baby in her arms, a bouncy toddler on one side and a quiet infant-school-aged boy, who until this moment had been neatly colouring in a picture of Santa, on the other.

Eyes like saucers, the boy grinned at Shipley. 'Hello,' he said.

Shipley ignored him, still staring at his mother.

Libby, embarrassed, called the dog. He glanced in her direction, but turned back, staring hard at the boy's mother.

The woman shifted in her seat. 'I've met your dog before,' she said, as Libby took a firm hold on Shipley's trailing lead. She should have done a better job of supervising him. 'I suppose you could say we're friends. We met in the vet's surgery – but I wish he'd stop staring at me. He's making me nervous.'

'Shipley. Sit.' To Libby's relief, he sank to the floor, one paw in the air. Libby reached out a hand to the little boy, a dog biscuit in her palm. 'Will you give Shipley a biscuit?'

He nodded, took the treat and held it out for Shipley.

The children in the carriage settled down again.

Libby returned to her seat, Shipley under firm control. 'I don't know what gets into him,' she told Joanna. 'He's had some training. We thought he might have a future as a police dog, but he's too strong-willed for that. He seems to have taken a real fancy to that lady. As if she doesn't have enough on her hands with all those children.'

'Mrs Atkins,' Joanna said.

She was interrupted by a burst of excited chatter in the carriage. One of the entertainers was pointing through the window. 'I can see Santa Claus,' she called.

The children rushed to the window and, sure enough, there he was, in costume, ringing a bell as the train drew into the station at the seaside town of Watchet.

15

BAA BAA BLACK SHEEP

Max found his Exham house lonely, that day, with Libby and the dogs all away. When he'd first moved in, he'd loved the space, and the peace and quiet. He'd furnished his study exactly as he wanted it, with a big mahogany desk that women, for some reason, hated. Libby had been dropping hints about 'letting the light in'. The man cave, she called it. It was said to be haunted.

For Max, that was part of its charm. Even Bear, after hesitation, had begun to enter the room, nervously. Presumably the ghost was friendly. Shipley had never found anything to worry him there.

When Libby was in the house, Max enjoyed retiring to his study, running his finger along the packed bookshelves, and stepping over the lengths of cables attached to his array of computers, monitors and audio equipment.

While she was away, he saw the room differently. He'd grown to like her cosy cottage, full of jars of flowers and the smell of baking, despite the cushions. Maybe the study could do with a little warming up, after all. A new rug, perhaps? He'd ask Libby.

He glanced at the calendar. Tomorrow was the first of December, and if it weren't for Libby's daughter, they'd be getting married in two weeks. Why couldn't Ali get here in time? Was it just selfishness?

Joe, his own son, had his faults, and they'd been angry with each other for many years after the divorce, but they'd been reconciled – mostly due to Libby's influence and a series of her home-cooked dinners. Nowadays, Joe and Claire were frequent, welcome visitors.

Max sighed. He wouldn't have to be patient for long. They were only putting the wedding back a week, to the twenty-second, and Libby had said the arrangements were well under way. The day would come soon enough, but meanwhile, Max needed to know Joe and Claire could be there.

He clicked on his email and wrote a few lines to his son. Libby had already told the small band of guests about the delay in the ceremony, so at least Max didn't have that task.

Just saying hi,

he wrote:

Any chance of you and Claire coming over for dinner in the next couple of days?

He should ask Robert, Libby's son, as well, with his wife, Sarah. They'd met Joe and Claire a few times, and they all seemed to get along well.

How about Sunday evening? I'll get Libby to cook up a storm, or feed you from the freezer if she can't face it! You can stay overnight, if you like.

Max's fingers hovered over the keys.

I saw your mother a few days ago. I'll tell you more when we meet.

No need to worry Joe about Stella's stalker. He was busy at work, with his new role in the Child Protection section in Hereford.

Max sent the email and turned to his inbox. A long list of marketing. He deleted most items with a satisfied flourish. He loved a clear inbox.

Stella's name caught his eye.

All well here,

she wrote.

Still in Bristol with Ivor. We've been sightseeing all over the Cotswolds. I've attached the lists you wanted. There are a few people we used to know in London, some good friends of mine and a few complete strangers.
I've highlighted the ones that could be weirdos.

Max was impressed with Stella's computing skills. Libby, for all her sharp intelligence, had even struggled to master the mobile phone. 'Chalk and cheese,' he muttered, wondering idly how the two women would get on together. Not well, he suspected.

He printed out Stella's list, and glanced at his inbox.

A new email had appeared that moment.

Baa Baa, Black sheep
Have you any wool?

Yes sir, yes, sir, three bags full.
One for the master
One for the dame
And one for the little boy who lived down the lane.

Well, well. Not only women being targeted, it seemed. That blew one of Max's theories out of the water. This was not a campaign run by a misogynist, designed to demean and frighten women.

But what did this email mean?

Black sheep – did that refer to Max? He'd made his share of mistakes in life, but they were personal, family issues. He hadn't so much as shoplifted a bar of chocolate during his youth or smoked a single cannabis cigarette.

Wool? Did that have any significance?

But, the master, a dame and a little boy; that could mean Max's previous family. If so, this was a nastier email than it appeared at first glance.

Someone could be reminding him of the past he'd messed up so badly.

More upset than he would have imagined, he wished Libby was here. But she was away on some school trip with the doctor's wife.

A daft idea came into Max's head. That Santa Special was going to Watchet. Why shouldn't he drive over there and meet her? It was time he offered some kind of romantic gesture.

He'd take the Land Rover, for the dogs were with Libby, and the four of them could spend the afternoon strolling near the harbour.

Fired with enthusiasm, and delighted to have a reason for leaving his depressingly empty house, he roared down the drive and pointed the car towards Bridgwater and the A39.

* * *

Watchet was one of Max's favourite Somerset towns. Just outside the Exmoor National Park, it didn't share much of the wealth brought by tourists, and it had suffered from the loss of the old paper mill that used to keep residents in work, but the locals seemed extraordinarily cheerful and optimistic. The marina had been redeveloped recently – maybe that would lead to the town's resurgence.

At least there was plenty of space to park. Max pulled into the car park close to the railway line, just as the train drew into the station with a noisy burst of steam, followed by the excited chatter of children.

'Ho, ho, ho.' Santa's laugh boomed out above the children's cheers as he beckoned them into the waiting room, miraculously transformed with holly, ivy, tinsel and trees, into Santa's Grotto.

He caught sight of Libby in conversation with a woman he supposed to be Joanna Sheffield. Max felt a grin spread across his face. Everything would be all right, now. His blues had vanished.

He'd walk down to the marina while Libby was talking, and enjoy a breath of bracing, fresh air.

He leaned on a bollard at the marina, the only soul there, watching the few boats that remained in the harbour as they bobbed on the tide. The others had been hauled on to dry land at the yacht club. What would it be like to own a boat? Max had never been sailing in his life, despite growing up in a seaside town. Maybe he'd try it, one of these days.

Lost in a daydream about sampling cocktails in a sparkling glass and chrome bar on the kind of yacht only a millionaire could afford, he didn't notice the man until he was at his elbow.

'Max?'

Max blinked.

'It's me.'

Recognition dawned. 'Ollie Redditch? You made me jump. What are you doing here?'

'Taking the air. Nice place, Watchet. Often come here. Long time, no see, though. What brings you out here?'

'I've come to collect Libby. She's with the Santa Special train crowd at the station.'

'I thought her kids were too old for Father Christmas.'

'She's with a friend and her children. The doctor's wife.'

Ollie grimaced. 'Stuck-up pair, that Joanna Sheffield and her husband. Think they're too good for Exham.'

Ollie had been at school with Max. Last time they'd met, in the Lighthouse pub in Exham a few years ago, Ollie had been full of beans, earning a small fortune from a slot machine arcade on the seafront.

'Women, eh?' Ollie went on. 'Drag you down, don't they? Take my ex-wife. Took me to the cleaners, good and proper, with the divorce,' Ollie grumbled. 'That was when Pritchards went bust and I lost my best little earner.' He winked. 'Strictly between ourselves, they used to send shedloads of lucrative work my way, hacking into their rivals' computers. All under the radar, of course. Put me back, it did, when they went bust. Still, you have to pick yourself up and carry on.'

Max grunted. Pritchards had been a shell company, running long-term fraud and money-laundering businesses that had tempted Libby's own husband into crime. Dismantling that business had been one of the earliest successes for Ramshore and Forest. He said, 'You were a bit of a whizz-kid, back in the seventies. We used to play Pong on the Atari, round your place. Do you remember?'

'Pong,' Ollie shook his head. 'Those were the days, when there were only a few of us games developers around. Games started me in the business. That's how I met the missus, down the arcade, more's the pity.'

'I'm sorry to hear about your wife,' Max said.

Ollie shrugged. 'Went off with some bloke running a casino in Weston-super-Mare, would you believe? At her age. Over the hill, she was, anyway, and I'd had enough of the nagging. Good riddance.'

Max recalled meeting Ollie's wife at a party, a few years ago. 'Ingrid, wasn't that her name?'

Ollie gave a short laugh. 'Never trust a Scandinavian.'

Ingrid had been – probably still was – a beautiful blonde. Ollie was still a good-looking man, although the jet-black hair had greyed and the handsome face with its chiselled cheekbones had gained a few wrinkles.

'Course, the doctor's not the only new arrival in Exham. You seen that Annabel Pearson?' Ollie chuckled and Max's heart sank.

When they'd been schoolboys, the whole gang of them – Ollie, Max, Bert, Alan Jenkins – had hung around Exham, eyeing up the girls arriving for their summer holidays. Resentful at being dragged to Somerset, when they'd rather have been stretched out in the sun on the beach in Spain or Portugal, the girls had been ready for romance with the local boys. Max had some great memories of those days, but he'd grown out of that method of meeting women. It seemed Ollie hadn't.

Ollie grinned. 'Still, business is getting back on track. I've opened a new place up in Bedwell, a virtual-reality games arcade. My aunt came up with a bob or two to start it. Now I'm in funds again, Annabel might be the next lucky girl.' He gave a wicked chuckle. 'She's working at that bakery with your Libby. I saw her there, yesterday. She's had one of those emails that are going around – you know, those nursery rhymes.'

Max nodded vaguely. He really didn't want to hear Ollie's crude opinion of Annabel.

'I got one, too,' Ollie added.

Now, he had Max's attention. 'You did?'

'Came this morning. Boys and girls come out to play, it was.' Ollie sniggered. 'Appropriate, don't you think?'

Whoever was sending the emails knew their audience.

Max wasn't about to tell Ollie he'd also been targeted. There was an awkward pause, broken, to his relief, by the noisy return of the children, clutching party bags and sucking on sweets.

'I'd better rescue Libby,' Max said, 'See you.'

16

FISH AND CHIPS

Max and Libby wandered through the narrow streets of Watchet, where every corner held an interesting smell that Shipley needed to investigate.

'I'm so glad you rescued me,' Libby said. 'I'd forgotten how exhausting small children can be. They loved Bear and Shipley, of course.'

'How was Father Christmas?' Max asked.

'Corpulent. Don't tell the children,' she made a show of peering over her shoulder, 'but under the whiskers and beard, I recognised William Halfstead.'

She took a step back to look at Max.

'Eyeing me up for next year?' he asked.

'Not fat enough.'

'Keep feeding me your bread and butter pudding and it won't be long before I am. Not sure I have the required jolly red face, either.'

'Maybe not. William really looked the part, though, and Margery was there as well, dressed as Mrs Claus and organising the children. So sad they never had any of their own.'

'Talking of children, have you heard from Ali again?'

Libby looked at the ground. 'Nothing new – she's pleased we're holding back the wedding.'

'So she should be.'

Libby didn't deny it. She linked her arm with his. 'You're being very understanding about the change of date. I did rather dump it on you.'

'So long as this is the last delay...'

'I promise.'

He took advantage of the moment, and told her he'd invited Joe and Claire to dinner.

She smiled. 'Great idea. I'm always pleased to see them. Of course, I'll cook. I haven't made beef wellington for months. Just the job for this weather. Speaking of which, I'm starving hungry after this morning's excitement. Where shall we eat?'

They looked around. 'Just cafés here, no posh restaurants,' Max said.

'But look,' Libby pointed across the road. 'A proper seaside fish and chip shop. What could be nicer? Who needs posh? And there's another Father Christmas.' They gazed up at the large red rear end of a plastic Santa poking out of a chimney on the roof.

Max said, 'I don't know why anyone who cooks as well as you do wants to eat chips.'

'Best thing ever, seaside chips with plenty of salt and vinegar. At least I don't smother my chips with mayonnaise. But let's get inside. The weather's getting colder by the minute. Do you think we'll have snow?'

He laughed. 'No chance, I'm afraid.'

They pushed open the door, and breathed in the familiar chip-shop smell.

As they ate melt-in-the mouth fish and vinegary chips, the dogs lying quietly under the table, they compared notes.

Libby described her conversation with Joanna Sheffield. 'Those children of hers are far too well-behaved. I longed to see them with chocolate smeared all over their faces, but Joanna kept cleaning them up.'

'I've met the doctor a couple of times,' Max said. 'Socially, I mean. Don't look so worried. I haven't had a doctor's consultation for years. I bumped into him in the Lighthouse, one evening. Big bloke, full of himself. I didn't take to him at all.'

'That sounds about right. Joanna's fine once you get to know her, although she talks about the children all the time. But you do when you have young ones, don't you?' She made a thinking face. 'The boy has his father's name – a bit old-fashioned, that. I bet it was the doctor's idea. I'm pleased to say the child insists on being called Jay instead of Jeremy.'

'Good for him. Did Joanna throw any light on her email?'

'Not really. But one thing's very clear – she's no friend of Annabel Pearson. She sounded quite spiteful; called Annabel the Merry Widow.' She paused. 'I've had an idea. If Joanna's right, and Annabel likes men more than women, why don't you talk to her about the email? I'm sure she'll melt under your charms.'

'Why not? I'm sick of background research into my ex-wife's friends, and I haven't found anything yet, except that she knows plenty of men. Apparently, she goes to the ballet with someone called Philip, visits stately homes with a Derek, and sings in a community choir with John. Which is crazy, because she can hardly hold a tune.'

'I'm beginning to think I'd like to meet your ex-wife.'

'Be careful what you wish for.' The idea horrified Max. 'You don't want her in your life, and nor do I.'

'Now,' Libby said, wiping her mouth on a paper napkin. 'Let's pay a visit to that funny little museum on the seafront. I've never been in. I suppose you know it from childhood.'

'You'll love it,' Max promised, and led the way to the Market House Museum, a glass-fronted building set on a sharp corner next to the quay.

They pushed open the door. The museum was open but deserted, except for a single woman, seated behind a table covered with shells, small replicas of anchors, old photographs and a couple of fossils.

'Come in, come in,' she beamed. 'Yes, and bring those lovely dogs. Everyone's welcome in here. I'm just sitting in while Quentin Dobson, the curator, popped out for lunch, so don't ask me any tricky questions, will you?' She held out a leaflet. 'Here's something about the history of the place.'

Obediently, Libby and Max read the short description.

The woman said, 'Haven't I seen you before? Mrs Forest, isn't it? I've been in your bakery and eaten your chocs. Hence the tummy.'

Max looked at her more closely. Was that a dog collar peeping out from under her crew neck sweater?

'You're the new vicar,' he said.

'Guilty as charged. Amy Fisher's the name.'

Max managed not to make the joke, but the wide grin on Libby's face gave the game away, and Amy Fisher hooted.

'Exactly. Fisher of men – very biblical, isn't it? I should have thought about that before I married my husband, shouldn't I? But I wasn't a vicar, in those days.' She waved a hand vaguely towards the shelves. 'I can't tell you everything about Watchet, I'm afraid. I'll leave that to Quentin. My proper place is up there.' She pointed to the ceiling. 'Upstairs, I mean, in Holy Cross Chapel. Our place of worship shares this building with the museum. Unusual, isn't it? Ah, and here's Quentin.'

Quentin Dobson, a small, bent man of at least seventy, peered at Libby and Max through half-moon glasses. 'Well, well, so nice to have visitors at this time of year. Thank you, Amy, for holding the fort.'

The cheerful vicar waved and departed, presumably to visit her domain. Sure enough, Max could soon hear footsteps above his head.

'Now, was there anything in particular you're interested in?'

Libby looked around. 'That's quite a collection of fossils you have here.'

'Ah, yes. Visitors often think they have to go to Lyme Bay, down in Dorset, to see fossils, but we have hundreds in this area.'

'Kilve,' Max said. 'I've been there, many times, when I was a boy.' He'd loved stepping with care over the limestone pavement, fingering the ammonites that covered many of the rocks and pocketing devil's fingernails.

Libby said, 'I've never been.'

The curator wagged a bony finger. 'A treat in store for you. But it's not just about the fossils. We pride ourselves on featuring the real history of the area. Are you fond of history?'

Max said, 'Libby's a shining light in the Exham History Society.'

Quentin Dobson's eyes gleamed above his glasses. 'Then, come this way, my dear. There's so much to show you. Let me put the kettle on and we'll have a lovely cup of tea. Milk and sugar?'

Two hours later they were still chatting happily with Quentin Dobson when Amy Fisher put her head around the door. 'Good gracious me. How wonderful to find folk so interested in our little town.'

Libby said, 'We've had a fascinating time. I've asked Mr Dobson to give a talk at the Exham on Sea History Society. I'll talk to the organiser, Angela Miles, but I know she's had a cancellation for next week's meeting.'

'If you want to know anything about Watchet, he's certainly

your man. I just called in to tell you it's time for the museum to
close. Quentin would sit here for hours if I didn't remind him.'

The curator looked at his watch. 'Good heavens. How time
flies.'

As they left, Max murmured in her ear, 'There isn't a meeting
next week.'

'I know.' She chuckled. 'But he was so happy talking to us, I
couldn't resist. I know Angela will agree. Meanwhile, these dogs
have behaved so well, I think they deserve a walk right around
the bay,' and she set off down the esplanade, Max and the dogs
trotting happily behind.

17

CHOCOLATE CAKE

Max spent the next morning reviewing Stella's list of Facebook friends, divided into three groups: the ten people known to both Stella and Max, some friends Stella sent comments to occasionally, and some complete unknowns. Not many of her friends appeared to be women.

After a glance at their pages, he discarded some self-described 'Generals' in the USA, whose pages consisted entirely of photographs of themselves. Max wondered what they were after, assumed it was easy sex, and moved on.

Taking the names of people Stella knew reasonably well, he scanned the information available on the site before carrying out a Google search. He found businessmen, a politician, and a handful of men he'd worked with in the bank, who'd taken early retirement. Stella showed a clear preference for wealth.

Among the names of people he recognised, one stood out. Angus. Angus and Hilary Margetson had often eaten supper with Max and Stella. They were no longer married, according to Facebook, and Angus's page included a photo of himself with Stella.

That was odd.

Digging deeper into Angus's background, Max found other photos of him with Stella. From the clothes and haircuts, it was clear they were taken long ago – before Max's divorce.

He sat back. He'd thought the problems between himself and Stella had all stemmed from Debbie's death. Stella had blamed him for arguing with Debbie that fateful day. The quarrel, trivial enough, about Debbie's timekeeping, had somehow escalated until Debbie had flounced out of the house, gone for a ride on her pony, fallen off and died. Max had never rid himself of the guilt, and Stella had agreed it was all his fault.

No marriage, he'd thought at the time, could withstand that.

Yet, here was evidence that Stella had already been spending time alone with Angus. Had they been having an affair?

Max's heartbeat slowed as he considered their life together.

He'd met Stella in his first week as a new graduate in the London bank. She'd been in the marketing department, working with magazines, newspapers, photographers and, as television became ever more sophisticated, producers of TV advertisements. She'd been beautiful, rich and popular, and Max, from the small, quiet backwater of Exham on Sea, with a degree from Exeter University in the West Country, had been dazzled.

In his heart, he'd always suspected she'd been unfaithful, but he'd chosen to close his eyes to the evidence – the times when she wasn't at home, the flimsy excuses for sudden days out, and once or twice, a weekend away 'with an old friend from school'.

It was time to be honest with himself. He'd lost Stella long before Debbie's death.

At least his parents, who'd never trusted her, had died before they'd been proved right.

Max needed air. Dipping into the morass of his old life threatened to suffocate him.

He took the dogs out and threw tennis balls for Shipley until his hands were too cold to continue. 'Come on, boys, let's get back inside.'

Back in the study, he laid logs in the grate, tucked firelighters in among them and, defying his own self-inflicted ban on daytime fires, took his laptop to the most comfortable chair in the room where he could watch the flames leaping up the chimney as he reviewed the other men on Stella's list.

He didn't notice the passage of time, until his stomach growled. He'd worked well past lunchtime. Discarding people whose updates Stella had liked or commented on recently, meaning they were on reasonably good terms, he'd whittled the list of men he'd consider suspects down to five, including Philip, Derek and John, men who'd featured in Stella's life recently, and Angus.

There was no guarantee any one of these had been stalking Stella, but they were a starting point. Was one of these men, all past boyfriends, angry enough with her to try to scare her? How could he find out?

Maybe it was time to bring in Joe. He was, after all, an experienced police officer. Younger than Debbie, he'd lived with his mother after the divorce. He might know some of these men.

Max couldn't wait for dinner on Sunday evening to raise the subject, and in any case, Libby's son and daughter-in-law would also be present. Max had no desire to wash his family's dirty linen in front of them.

He rang Joe, pleased to find that his son had a spare hour, later that day.

* * *

The drive to Hereford that afternoon reminded Max of his search for Bear, a few short weeks ago. For once, he was alone, the dogs snoring quietly at home. Max had been tempted to ask Libby to come, but she was busy in the shop, letting Mandy start her weekend early, preparing for Steve's arrival.

Joe had suggested they meet in a tiny tea shop he'd visited before.

The waitress remembered Max. That soothed his bruised ego a little.

Trained by Libby, he took an intelligent interest in the cakes on offer at the counter, and managed a gentle banter with the waitress over the relative merits of coffee and walnut, or chocolate layer cake.

Joe arrived as Max agreed to try both.

Joe's eyes, as blue as Max's own, sparkled. 'Flirting, Dad?' he mocked.

'Just passing the time of day.'

As Joe poured tea into two chintzy cups, Max described his meeting with Stella, and her worries about a stalker.

Joe nodded. 'She told me. She said, don't bother you about it. She's not worried.'

'What? You know?' What was Stella playing at? She'd told Max she was scared.

'How long have you known?' he asked.

'She rang, last weekend. She didn't say she was coming down to Bristol, though. Didn't want to visit me, maybe. She doesn't get on with Claire.'

Max chuckled. Claire, Joe's wife, was a clinical psychologist, and nobody's fool. 'Does that bother you?'

'Dad, we both know Mum's a bit – well – flaky. I love her to bits, and she's a hoot at a party once she's had a gin and tonic, but I've learned never to be surprised – or embarrassed – by anything she says or does. I suspect this stalker story's some chancer, targeting any woman he can find. Ivor's been looking into it for a while. Don't you think all this desire for your help's blown up at a convenient time, just as you're about to get married again?'

'You mean she's jealous?'

'Course she is.' Joe leaned across and took a forkful of Max's chocolate cake. 'Honestly, Dad, for a man with an analytical mind, you're pretty dim sometimes when it comes to people.'

Max sat back, chewing thoughtfully, thinking that over. Reluctantly, he came to the conclusion there was some evidence that Joe was right. For one thing, trying to keep his meeting with Stella secret had been a stupid idea. He'd completely misunderstood Libby's possible reaction.

Then, his old friend, Angus, from their London years, had turned out not to be a friend at all. All those pints with the man, the times the two couples had eaten at each other's houses, and Max hadn't felt the slightest suspicion Angus and Stella were having a fling.

He switched his attention back to Joe, who'd finished eating.

'The waitress is right about this cake. Almost – but not quite – as good as Libby's.' Joe checked his watch. 'Sorry, Dad. Got to run. Places to go, villains to catch. See you on Sunday for dinner. Tell Libby we can't wait – we'll be skipping lunch so we can do justice to her food. Meanwhile, I'll take these names and do some digging, but I think we'll find you're worrying unnecessarily.'

He thumped Max on the shoulder and left.

Max sat alone for a while. What was really going on? Had Stella been leading him up the garden path with this so-called stalker, or were her emails genuine? And if they were, was there any connection with the Exham nursery rhymes? His internet searches had failed to find any sort of nursery rhyme hoaxes or memes sweeping social media.

A very unpleasant inkling of an idea arrived at the back of his mind, and began to take root.

Libby's Saturday shift at Brown's Bakery was due to start early, so the Citroen chose that morning to refuse to start.

Furious, she revved the engine, jabbed at the clutch and swore loudly, before abandoning the car outside Hope Cottage. She transferred to the red Hyundai she'd bought for the business, that Mandy used for marketing and delivery trips around the county. Thank heaven it was Saturday so Mandy didn't need it.

Before she left, Libby scribbled an apologetic note. She wouldn't see much of her lodger over the next few days, while Steve was back in town.

A queue was already forming outside Brown's Bakery when she arrived, and Frank was bringing the first loaves of the day through to the front of the shop. They steamed, still hot from the oven.

Alan Jenkins was first in the queue. 'Morning, Libby,' he said. 'Have you thought any more about that little car I told you about?'

'Funny you should say that.' Libby told him about the Citroen's refusal to start.

'Probably the cold weather overtaxing the battery,' Alan pronounced. 'Affects an old jalopy like yours, and it's brass monkey weather, today. Why don't I call around later and take a look? It may just need a battery boost.'

Libby nodded towards the line of hungry Exham folk. 'When all this has died down and Frank's back from his deliveries? Annabel will be in later.' She consulted the list, pinned to a board at the back of the shop. 'I have a couple of cakes to take out to Nether Stowey early this afternoon. Can you call in after that – I'll have my head in the oven, cooking. The family are coming for a meal, tomorrow.'

Her heart lifted as she spoke. Robert and Sarah, plus Joe and Claire – and Ali would be here before long. The wedding arrangements were coming along nicely, and she'd repaired that strange disconnect with Max. They were back on the same wavelength, although he'd been a little quiet and thoughtful when he returned from seeing Joe.

Joanna Sheffield was last in the line of customers.

Libby greeted her with a wide smile. 'That was a great outing on Thursday. The children loved it, didn't they?'

Joanna didn't meet her gaze, pointing instead to the last couple of loaves on the shelf. 'Don't you have any cobs left? The ones with sesame seeds?'

'All gone, I'm afraid. How about that cottage loaf? It's very similar.'

Joanna frowned. 'Jeremy likes the cob.'

Jeremy would have to lump it, or get up early and buy the bread himself.

Soothingly, Libby said, 'We can set up a delivery for you. Frank likes to get out of the shop in the mornings, and you don't live far away.'

Joanna shook her head. 'I like to come into town.'

Libby looked more closely. Joanna's eyes were red-rimmed, as though she'd been crying, or was very tired.

'Is everything all right?' Libby asked.

'Fine, thank you. I'm a little tired. The children, you know.' Joanna kept her eyes firmly on her hands as she packed the loaf, in its paper bag, into a shopping bag.

Before Libby could enquire further, Gladys arrived. Joanna brushed past, on her way to the door, and left without another word. Libby watched her go.

Gladys said, 'No manners, that one. Thinks she's a cut above the rest of us, she does. What with her and that Annabel, I don't know what the town's coming to.' Gladys seemed cheerful enough, today, despite her sister's death. In fact, she could hardly stand still, but jigged up and down in front of the counter. 'The solicitor rang me yesterday to tell me Carys left me some money,' she burst out, as though unable to keep her news to herself for a moment longer. 'A bit of a windfall, for me. Who'd have thought it?'

'That's nice.'

Gladys nodded her head so vigorously that Libby wondered if she'd do herself a mischief. 'The solicitor says it's too early to know the full amount, what with probate and bank accounts and so on, but she left a will, you see, and I'll be getting at least one hundred thousand pounds, probably a lot more. And that's before selling her little holiday home in Powys. I'll have enough to put down a deposit on a place of my own, and I can let out that flat over the shop, make a spot of income for my old age.'

'Good for you,' Libby said.

'Well, you could have knocked me down with a feather when he rang. I thought Carys was stony broke. She came to stay with me for her holidays last year, because she couldn't afford anything better. Or, so she said. Seems she picked up a bob or two from those divorces of hers.'

Libby handed over Gladys' change. 'Maybe she just liked visiting Exham?'

'Or someone in the town, more like,' Gladys said, with a broad wink.

* * *

Max wasn't at all sure he wanted to meet Annabel Pearson alone. Her nickname, the Merry Widow, was worrying for a man about to get married and already under pressure from his ex-wife. It was great that Libby trusted him, of course.

'Women,' he said to Shipley, who was panting hard, sensing the possibility of a walk, or at the very least, a ride in the car. 'I'll never understand them.'

On balance, he'd decided, the best thing was to meet Annabel in a public place. Not the beach. Max enjoyed his walks with Libby and the dogs too much to walk there with anyone else.

'Maybe I'm a romantic old fool, after all, Ships.'

As it turned out, when he'd rung her yesterday, to explain his official links to the police and to ask if they could meet, Annabel had made a better suggestion. 'I'm taking Jamie, my son, to a session at the climbing wall in Bristol, tomorrow. He loves to climb, and I hate heights, so I'll be sitting by myself all morning. I'd love to talk to you instead.'

So, at nine o'clock that morning, Max bade a fond farewell to Bear and a disappointed Shipley, for he was sure the spaniel would become hopelessly overexcited in the noise and bustle of the leisure centre.

The centre teemed with children hopping with excitement,

while adults fixed their helmets and hooked them up to the equipment.

Annabel sat by the restaurant area, wearing some kind of furry jacket, with a cup of coffee in one hand. She'd piled coats on to a nearby chair, and as Max approached, she cleared them away. 'I managed to save you a seat. And a coffee. Hope you like latte.'

Max didn't really. He liked his coffee the old-fashioned way – filtered, as Libby served it, but at least this was warm. He balanced the lifetime cup she'd used on his knee as she said, 'Jamie has another half-hour here. The session's limited, so it's all very safe.' She pointed to a boy halfway up a ten-foot wall. 'There he is, loving it. It terrifies me.'

She smiled at Max with dazzling white teeth, her eyes shining as though he was the one person in the world she wanted to talk to above all others.

How do people do that? Max smiled in return, hoping he wasn't blushing, glad Libby wasn't there to laugh.

Annabel said, 'What do you think of that Christmas tree?' An enormous, tinsel-covered artificial tree reached from the floor to the roof of the cavernous building.

'Wow,' Max said.

'Yes. It puts the bakery in the shade. We put up a few baubles yesterday, to brighten the place up, but it will be closed before Christmas. The new café, though – it's going to be wonderful.'

Annabel had a sparkle in her eyes. She looked as though she was settling in to Exham more easily than Libby had suggested.

Max managed to collect his thoughts. 'I wanted to talk to you because you had an anonymous email. Libby and I work with the police, and they asked us to look into these rhymes.'

Annabel's smile faded. 'To be honest, I was flattered, at first. I mean, who minds being called the Queen of Hearts? But then, I started to wonder. How did the Rhymer know my email address?

Was it someone I know? When I think about it, I feel quite sick. The Rhymer could be creeping around Exham, watching us all secretly.' She shook her head. 'And Carys died.' Her hand trembled a little as she sipped her coffee. 'I keep checking the doors and windows at home, and looking behind me. To tell you the truth, I'm almost regretting the move to Exham.'

Annabel's eyes were wide and very blue. Max could see why men liked her and wanted to protect her, and why women were less keen. Fortunately, Annabel wasn't his type at all. She reminded him of a nervous rabbit. 'So, you don't have any idea who might have sent it?'

She shook her head. 'I gather it's untraceable.'

'Have you received any other strange emails?'

She thought for a moment. 'Just the usual ones telling me to click on a link to win a prize, or that I need to change my bank account number. So far, I haven't fallen for any of the scams, although they get cleverer all the time, don't they? My aging mother lives alone, in one of these apartments for elderly people on the seafront in Exham. She prides herself on using a laptop, and I do worry someone might trick her. She thinks everyone is kind and honest.' She broke off to wave at Jamie, who'd reached the top of the wall and was wind-milling his arms in delight. 'I wish she'd come and live with Jamie and me, but she's far too independent. I'd like her company, to be honest. It's lonely, being a single parent, and Jamie's growing up fast, with all that means.'

Max offered a sympathetic grin. 'Long silences, grunts at breakfast, constant fights over smelly trainers. I remember it well, although my son's grown up now. You moved to Exham recently?'

'We used to live in Gloucester. My husband Liam was in the army. He died in Afghanistan, but I stayed on in the area. The trouble with the army is, once you're no longer part of it, all your friends disappear. They don't mean to, but they move away, posted to other places, and one day, I found I wasn't just missing Liam, but everyone I used to know, and I was lonely. Married couples didn't really like to have me around. Competition for the wives.' Her eyes sparked with a small flash of anger. 'Some of them don't trust their husbands around a single woman.'

Max nodded.

She went on, 'My parents came to Exham ten years ago, before my father died. They'd always wanted to retire to the seaside, and my mother loves it.'

'But you don't?'

'No, it's too small for me. I hoped to become part of the community, but most people don't want to know. Or at least...' She stopped, a tiny smile at the corners of her mouth.

Max said, 'Libby found the same thing, when she arrived. It took a while for her to find her feet.'

'When she met you, I imagine?' Annabel was smiling. Was she flirting?

Max cleared his throat. 'Anyway,' he said. 'Working in the bakery's a good idea. You'll meet everyone there.'

'The local gossips, at least.' At that moment, her son arrived. She murmured, 'Please, don't say anything to Jamie about the emails. I don't want to worry him.'

Her face had lit up as he arrived, but Jamie stood with folded arms and a glum expression.

'Well done, darling,' Annabel enthused.

Jamie shifted from one foot to the other.

'This is Mr Ramshore. Say hello.'

Jamie looked Max up and down. 'Hello,' he grunted. 'Do you climb?'

'Afraid not,' Max admitted.

'My dad could. He could climb anything. He was in the marines.'

'Was he?'

The boy nodded. 'He could take anyone, if he wanted. He was a boxer.'

Annabel interrupted. 'Jamie, really. Dad wouldn't want you to talk like that.'

The boy's lip curled. 'How do you know?'

'Jamie!'

Hoping to smooth things over, Max said, 'What other sports do you do?'

The boy counted on his fingers. 'Cricket, swimming, rugby – though they don't play properly at my new school. I was the best half-back in my old team.' He glared at his mother.

Max said, 'You miss it?'

'Exham kids are wimps.'

That attitude wasn't going to help his mother find friends.

'Well, I have to be going.' Max smiled at Annabel.

As he left, he heard Jamie's voice. 'So, what did that old man want then?'

Annabel had her hands full with that boy. And Max hadn't discovered anything about the mysterious emails. He'd stick to his computer, in future, and leave the personal interviews to Libby.

'Ten for dinner.' Libby stood in the kitchen at Max's house on Sunday evening. 'It's a while since we've gathered everyone together like this. It's been a hectic afternoon, getting everything ready, but I think it's all done. I'm looking forward to this evening. Especially as Angela's bringing Owen with her. The only one missing is Reg. He's back in America.' She tied her apron tightly over her little black dress. 'Just as well, I think, as Steve's coming with Mandy. She had a soft spot for Reg at one time. Not surprising, I have to say. What a man.'

She grinned at Max to make it clear she hadn't really fallen for the tall, handsome American, despite his shaved head, slow drawl and basketball-player's physique.

Max was riffling through the cutlery drawer. 'What's on the menu? I don't want to get the table settings wrong. Is there soup to follow the starter? Or, perhaps,' he affected a cut-glass accent, 'a tiny amuse-bouche to begin, or a gelato to cleanse the palate between courses?'

'Are you mocking me?' Libby threw a tea towel in Max's direction. 'I know better than to give our children anything they'd call fancy food – or you, for that matter. In fact, there's a dip to eat with the pre-dinner drinks, while I panic in the kitchen. Then, it's tomato and garlic bruschetta, followed by that beef wellington you can smell in the oven, with lots of roast vegetables, including Brussels sprouts, by the way, but you don't have to eat those. They're Robert's favourite vegetable, weirdly. Then, there's cauliflower wellington for vegetarians. By which I mean just Claire, unless she's won Joe over?'

'Not likely. And, what's for pudding?'

'You and your sweet tooth. You have to guess. What would you like?'

'Not bread and butter pudding, I suppose?'

'No. You can't have that every day. Guess again.'

Max sidled across the room and flung open the fridge. 'I knew it. Chocolate mousse.'

'Mandy would never eat anything else if she could help it. How does all that sound?'

'Like manna from heaven.'

* * *

Angela and Owen were first to arrive, bearing wine and chocolates, and within twenty minutes, the house was filled with the laughter of friends and family.

Libby, her apron consigned to a hook on the back of the kitchen door, wondered if it were possible to feel any happier without actually bursting. Even the Citroen was running again, after Alan had given the battery a boost. He'd shaken his head, sucked his teeth and insisted the car wouldn't last much longer. It was definitely time for an upgrade. Libby would be sad to see her purple friend go.

Max poured wine. Robert and Sarah avoided the alcohol.

'We've been drinking Beck's Beer,' Robert said. Alcohol-free, Libby noted.

She exchanged a glance with Angela, who was watching Sarah, her eyes like saucers. An idea struck Libby. Deciding to keep her mouth shut for the moment, she served the bruschetta and waited.

Soon it was time for the main course.

'Sarah and Robert, would you like to try this rather special Pinot Noir I've brought up from the cellar?' Max asked. 'Well, from the rack in the kitchen, anyway.'

Robert and Sarah looked at each other and burst out laughing.

'You've guessed, haven't you?' Sarah said.

Libby clasped her hands together as Robert rose to his feet. Surely not – it would be too good to be true.

'I have an announcement,' he said, holding his glass of alcohol-free beer. 'Sarah and I are pregnant.'

Tears started in Libby's eyes, and she had to bite her lip to steady it. A baby in the family!

On the other side of the table, Claire smiled brightly, but her cheerful expression soon faded, and Joe's congratulations sounded subdued.

Was there a problem there?

Now wasn't the time to pry. Instead, Libby toasted her son and his wife, muttering to herself, 'A granny. I'm going to be a granny.'

She hardly tasted the rest of the meal – not even the chocolate mousse.

As Mandy suggested baby names, each one more ridiculous than the last, 'What's wrong with Chardonnay?' Max brought coffee through from the kitchen to the dining room. As he set the tray down, his phone dinged with a message.

He shook his head. 'That can wait, whatever it is.'

A second later, Joe's phone rang. Silence fell on the room. Max and Joe looked at each other, and a cold shiver ran down Libby's spine.

'You'd better take it,' she said.

The colour drained from Joe's face. He dropped the phone onto the table. 'That was Ivor. Mum's in hospital in Bristol.'

* * *

As Max arrived at the Bristol hospital early the next morning, and asked for Stella's room number, a bulky individual with pointy shoes, close-cropped hair, and a physique that had to owe its strength to constant workouts, appeared at his shoulder. This must be Ivor Wrighton, Stella's latest partner, a man twenty years younger than she was.

Ivor held out his hand, a flashy gold watch catching the early-morning sun that shone, low on the horizon, grazing the Bristol skyline.

'You must be Max.' Ivor's smooth face barely creased. Botox? Or just the flexibility of youth.

Max didn't really care. They were never going to be best friends. 'And you're Ivor.' They shook hands. That was enough small talk for Max. 'How is she?'

'She'll be OK. Swallowed tablets – not too many, luckily. She's done it before.'

'Really?'

She'd self-medicated with whisky in the past, but Max hadn't known she had a bad relationship with pills.

'When did you get here? I'd assumed you'd both gone home to Surrey.'

'I had to get back, see to some business. In fact,' he grinned at Max in a man-to-man way that set Max's teeth on edge. 'We had a bit of a barney, to be honest. Stella wanted me to stay on here, and refused to come back to Surrey. I came back yesterday, after the police phoned me.'

Max had forgotten she was staying on in Bristol with this man.

'Yes,' Ivor's smile didn't reach his eyes. 'We'd planned to spend a few days in the area, but I couldn't stay long. I think this business with the tablets was just a spot of attention-seeking.'

Max was speechless. How could Stella bear to live with this man?

'I'll show you the way to her room. It's a rabbit warren, here.' Ivor walked ahead of Max through apparently interminable hospital corridors, following signs, and lines painted on the floor leading to one of the medical wards in the private wing of the hospital. Ivor stopped at the entrance to the ward. 'I'll leave the two of you alone. Back in half an hour.'

Ivor turned and walked back the way they'd come. As Max stepped into Stella's room, he caught sight of Ivor stopping to talk to one of the nurses. A pretty blush rose to the young girl's cheeks.

Grinding his teeth, Max turned back to the private room, and Stella.

Lying in bed, Stella looked her age in spite of the fact that her hair was already neatly combed.

She raised one hand in a weak gesture. 'Come in,' she murmured. 'I'm over the worst.'

A great weariness overwhelmed Max. He wished he could be anywhere else in the world. 'What did you think you were doing?'

She smiled, her lips trembling as she touched a handkerchief delicately to her eyes. 'I didn't mean to cause trouble. I just felt so – alone.'

'You'd quarrelled with Ivor. He told me.'

'Dear Max.' She moved her hand again, the gesture reminding Max of a film he'd seen – black and white, historical, set when ladies swooned and wept. All Stella needed was a fan to complete the picture. 'I know you can't understand. Life's so good for you, with Libby.'

'But, your quarrel with Ivor wasn't serious, was it?'

She offered another gentle smile. 'Silly Ivor. He's a dear, but he's no replacement for a real man. He couldn't even be bothered to stay with me here. I've been alone in Bristol for days.' She struggled to sit. 'Could you just plump up my pillow a little?'

Max complied, keeping his face blank.

'I'm so sorry, Max. I won't do anything so stupid again. I was – just so sad.'

Max wished he was in Exham, with Libby, away from all his ex-wife's dramas. After the bombshell had dropped last night, Claire had driven Joe to see Stella, insisting Max should wait until today. He'd then spent a restless, guilt-fuelled night, imagining this was his fault.

What was it Ivor had said? She'd done it before? Max wished he'd brought Libby along. She'd offered to come, volunteering to stay in the car while he saw his ex-wife, but, like a fool, he'd refused. His ex-wife was his problem, and he should sort it out himself. If only he didn't feel so hopelessly out of his depth.

'What brought it on this time?' he asked.

Stella's eyes flickered. Surprised he knew this wasn't the first time she'd taken an overdose?

Max asked, 'Is it to do with my marriage?'

'No, Max. It isn't. How very like you to think everything's about you. No, it was the email. You see, another one arrived and it was too much for me. Someone's after me. I can't spend my life looking behind, cowering at home, wondering if this stalker's going to hurt me. Who wants to live life like that? I just wanted to end it, once and for all.' That had to be genuine distress in her eyes, alongside the drama.

Max concentrated on the facts. 'Another email?'

'It was different; a silly rhyme, but I'm sure it came from the same person.'

A chill brought the hairs on Max's neck to attention. 'You mean, a nursery rhyme?'

'Goosey Goosey Gander. Do you know it?'

Max dredged his memory.

> 'Goosey Goosey Gander
> Where shall I wander?
> Upstairs and downstairs
> And in my lady's chamber.'

'That's it,' Stella said. 'I was terrified. I already knew someone was coming after me, but this time – in my lady's chamber? I don't want to go home but I know you're too busy to help, what with the arrangements for your wedding.'

The old, familiar wave of self-reproach swept over Max. Stella had asked him for help with her stalker, he hadn't taken it seriously enough, and the stalker had ramped up the threat level.

'Did the email ask for anything? Any sort of blackmail? Did it say, pay up or I'll tell people about your past?'

Stella raised a chilly eyebrow. 'There is nothing to be ashamed of in my past.'

Ivor arrived back at that moment. 'Well, you're looking a bit more chipper,' he told Stella, clapping a pair of large, meaty hands together. 'We'll soon have you out of here. Let's forget about the hotel, go home and get a few friends round. Have a bit of a party. That'll cheer you up.'

If Max were to speak like that to Libby, she'd have something to say, but Stella giggled like a teenager, forgetting she'd said she was too scared to go home. 'I've been silly, haven't I?'

'You certainly have. You need to lighten up. Don't take life so seriously.'

The man handled Stella with ease. She seemed besotted with him. When Max said he'd leave the two of them alone, she hardly glanced his way.

As he left, Max spoke to the sister in charge of the ward. 'We take every suicide attempt very seriously,' she said. 'Her partner, Mr Wrighton, is arranging for her to see a psychiatrist privately, so she's going to be discharged later today. As you can see, we're rushed off our feet in here, and we need her bed.'

Max drove back to Exham, longing to discuss the whole mess with Libby, and wondering how he could possibly keep Stella safe. He hadn't taken to Ivor Wrighton one little bit.

* * *

'What if Ivor's the stalker?' Libby was plying Max with tea and cake, the dogs curled at his feet, as though in sympathy.

'I've been wondering about that, but it doesn't make sense. He seems keen to make Stella happy. He came to Bristol as soon as he heard she was in hospital, and he's planning to take her home and look after her. She seems pleased as punch at the idea. He's almost half her age, rippling with muscles, apparently rich and covered in bling, so I suppose he offers everything she needs.'

Libby said, 'It sounds to me as though they're playing games with each other. You're well out of it, Max. Don't let it get to you.'

'Hmm.'

'Why's he so keen to be with an older woman?' Libby asked.

Max shrugged. 'Toy boys and cougars – it's not uncommon, these days.'

'Unless he's after her money?'

'He seems to have plenty of his own, judging by the bling on his wrist. I shall dig around in his background a little, but meanwhile, we need to rethink these emails. They make less sense every time I think about them. Sometimes, fraud and phishing emails are just random. The criminal gets hold of passwords, from lists for sale on the black web. They're easy to find if you know where to look, and not even expensive. Then, the perpetrator sends out emails, telling the recipients he's hacked their machines and can see everything they're getting up to. It's usually about porn sites, but that doesn't work if the recipient's a woman.'

'Unless they have photos online they wouldn't want anyone to see.'

'Naked, you mean?'

'Or worse.'

Max tapped a teaspoon on the table as he thought. 'These emails are targeted in a more personal way than that, though. Whoever's sending them seems to know a good deal about their victims. Annabel's seen as a bit of a threat to other women, and Mandy has a Little Red Riding Hood cloak. Then, there's Carys Evans' bad reputation.'

'And that's where it gets serious.' Libby was frowning. 'Carys was killed, which puts a whole different light on this. She's the only person who's died so far, but we have to take the threats seriously. Everyone who received one of the nursery rhyme emails needs to take care.'

'But the stalker can't be planning to kill them all at once. There are at least five that we know of, including myself and Ollie, that old mate of mine from school, and probably a few more. Not everyone will tell, especially if the rhyme hits home too hard. And don't forget, Carys' email arrived after she'd already died.'

Libby had been holding her breath. She let it out in a long sigh. 'So, the next victim could be anyone. We have hardly any clues at all, except those Facebook friends of Stella's. Between us, we've talked to everyone who's admitted to receiving the emails and none of them has admitted to knowing any reason why they've been targeted. In fact, they're all reluctant to take them seriously. Even Gladys thinks they're just a bad joke. She reckons Carys had a fight with one of her men friends, who lost his temper.'

Max said, 'No, that's not how it happened. There's no evidence of a struggle, according to Morrison. He thinks someone crept up on Carys and bopped her on the head deliberately, out of the blue.'

'Which makes it cold-blooded. A contract killing? But why? Who had anything to gain, except Gladys, and I can't believe she either did it herself or paid someone else, just to get her hands on a hundred thousand pounds.'

Max said, 'We need to step up on this. I've printed out the photos of the men who seem most likely to be Stella's stalker. We can show them to everyone who's had a nursery rhyme, and see if they recognise them.'

Libby said, 'What was your rhyme? Anything that made sense?'

He cleared his throat. 'Baa Baa Black sheep. I think I can guess what it means – a reference to my family – my old family.'

Libby ran through the rhyme. '*One for the master, one for the dame, and one for the little boy who lives down the lane. You're the master, and Joe's the little boy, which, I suppose, makes Stella the dame.*'

'That's what I thought. I haven't mentioned it to her, by the way.'

'But it means you may be under threat as well. Who have you upset recently?'

Max burst out laughing. 'There are plenty of business frauds who hate me, because of the work I've done, but they're unlikely to know much about me personally.'

'Let's hope you're right. I assume you don't have an enemy amongst Stella's friends?'

'Not that I can think of, unless it's the wife of someone she had an affair with, and I really don't see how I can take the blame for that.'

20

BREAK IN

Libby spent the rest of Monday in the bakery. She took photo-copies of Stella's suspicious friends' images and showed them to Exham residents. Mandy roared with laughter. 'These old geezers? Never seen any of them. This one's fit, though.' She pointed to the photo of Ivor that Max had included.

'You'd better not let Max hear you say that. Ivor is his ex-wife's squeeze.'

'Her toy boy? Good for her. But don't tell Steve I said so. He's furious to be going back to London while all this is kicking off. He wanted to stick around and help discover the secret Nursery Rhyme Stalker. By the way, I was thinking about my rhyme.'

'Little Red Riding Hood.'

'Exactly. I wondered who it might be – you know, the wolf that eats the granny.'

'Who's the granny, for that matter? I don't think the stalker worries too much about the detail in the rhymes. They're designed to shock. He or she is playing games with us all.'

Angela arrived, carrying a new, fat briefcase.

Mandy crowed, 'Look at you, all business-like. I bet the

contractors working on the new café tremble when they see you coming.'

'I do hope so,' Angela said. 'Otherwise the work will never get done. They're geniuses at inventing reasons for delays. They rang this morning to say they've received the wrong kind of paint, so they can't do any work today. Last week, it was chipboard that was too thick, and tiles that were the wrong shade. I swear, it would be easier to fix the place ourselves.'

Libby spread egg mayonnaise on a row of baps. 'You're loving every moment of it, so stop pretending. Did Owen give you the briefcase?'

Angela blushed, but there was no time to talk further, as the lunchtime rush began.

No one recognised the men in the photographs, and no one had received any new suspicious emails, or any other kind of threat.

'Just the usual Monday,' Libby said to Mandy. 'It's almost dull.'

Freddy from the estate agents pricked up his ears. He'd become a regular customer, and Libby suspected he had set his sights on Mandy.

'You haven't heard, then?' he said.

'Heard what?' Mandy was feigning boredom.

'About Gladys. Someone broke into her shop last night. Wrecked the place, and left a note as well.'

Angela, Libby and Mandy shared astonished stares. 'We hadn't heard anything. What did the note say?'

'It said, "Unless you want the same as your sister, you'd better send £100,000 to... and some email address." What are you doing?'

Libby had grabbed her phone and was already talking to Max.

* * *

The flower shop was wrecked. Libby and Mandy stood outside the yellow police tape and watched the white-clad scenes of crime officers moving around just inside the gaping front door, searching for fingerprints and other evidence.

Gladys stood nearby, talking to DC Gemma Humberstone as PC Tim Green approached Libby.

'Er, Mrs Forest,' he muttered, looking at the ground. How was he ever going to manage as a police officer? 'Gemma – er – wondered if you'd come and talk to Ms Evans. She's very upset.'

Mandy whispered, 'You'd better fill us in later, Mrs F,' as, reluctantly, she returned to the bakery.

Libby, Gemma and Gladys perched on stools in the empty café.

Gladys held a crumpled tissue in one hand. 'Well, I never,' she repeated at intervals. 'Who would have thought they'd attack my poor little shop.'

'They?' Gemma asked. 'Do you know who "they" might be?'

'No idea,' Gladys twisted it the tissue into a damp pellet.

Gemma added, 'Why don't you tell us everything you know, and we'll take it from there.'

'Well,' Gladys scrubbed at her eyes, then pushed one of the tissues into her sleeve, 'I suppose it might be something to do with Carys. You see, she came to stay last year, and that's when all this seems to have begun.'

'Go on,' Gemma prompted.

'Carys took up with someone when she was here. A chap from Weston. Not one of her old boyfriends, another one.'

Gemma's eyes opened wide.

Libby said, 'Gladys' sister had rather a... a colourful background.'

Gladys nodded. 'Three husbands and plenty who never got that far. I reckon, one of them had the hump, hit Carys on the head and came to my shop to find something.'

'What would they have been looking for?'

'Money, I suppose.' Gladys looked about ready to cry again.

Libby said, 'You told me about your legacy from your sister. Don't you think it odd that this note is demanding the same sum of money as your inheritance?'

Gladys heaved a deep sigh and raised her hands as if in defeat. 'I suppose I ought to tell you. You see, Maurice, my nephew, that's Carys' son, he's been a bit of a chancer all his life. Only just on the right side of the law, and he stepped over that line once or twice. But Carys said he'd changed his ways. Changed his name as well, she said, when he came out of prison a while back. To be honest, I was surprised she didn't leave her money to him.

'Now, I've been away this weekend – I went on Friday to see the solicitor in Bath, and I stayed with a friend of mine for the weekend. First thing this morning, I went to the market for flowers, same as I always do on a Monday morning, loaded up the van and drove back to Exham. Well, I couldn't believe it when I found the state of my little shop. The lock on the front door broken, and inside, smashed vases everywhere. I could have kicked myself – I'd forgotten to turn on the burglar alarm when I left – I was still in a bit of a state about Carys, to be honest.'

As she tried to blow her nose on the damp remains of her tissue, Libby held out a new one.

Gladys went on, 'I reckon young Maurice came looking for money from me, on account of Carys not leaving him any, and when he couldn't find me, he trashed my lovely shop.'

As she talked, her Welsh accent became so pronounced that Libby and Gemma looked at each other in confusion.

Gemma said, 'Let me get this straight. You think Carys' son, Maurice, came looking for money, and destroyed your shop out of spite and to get you to hand over the money he thought should be his?'

'What other reason could there be?'

Libby asked, 'How about the note; the demand for money? Does it ask you to pay it in to a bank, or leave it anywhere?'

'We've collected that as evidence,' Gemma said. 'We can find out if the perpetrator left any DNA or fingerprints.'

'Will it be possible to track down the address for the payments or is it one of these anonymous IP destinations, like the one used for the nursery rhyme emails?'

Gemma said, 'We'll get one of our computer geniuses to track it, but the note asks for a Bitcoin payment and my guess is it will be almost impossible to track down the payments.'

Max spent Tuesday morning with the dogs, walking them gently in the fields. He let Bear set the pace and was watching him closely, relieved to see him moving more freely, when Libby called with news of the break-in.

'Gemma's on the case, trying to track down the email address, but she doesn't hold out much hope.'

'We need to look more closely at Carys' son, Maurice. I'm sure Morrison's team will get on to it, but I might be quicker.'

'And it's just the kind of job you like, chasing clues through the internet.'

'Exactly.'

Max turned for home as a burst of winter sunshine bathed the fields in a golden glow, matching his happier mood. With his usual, comfortable relationship with Libby restored, Stella in Ivor's charge, and Bear set for a few more happy, active years, life was getting back on track. If he and Libby could solve the riddle of the Nursery Rhymer, the path to their wedding would seem almost smooth.

The phone rang. Stella. His sunny mood evaporated.

His finger hovered in the air. Could he just decline the call, block her number and refuse to have anything else to do with her?

Of course, he couldn't.

He answered the call. 'Stella?'

She babbled, hysterical. 'Max. Max, you've got to help.' He could hardly hear a word through her sobs.

'Take a deep breath,' he said. 'Try to stay calm. Whatever's wrong, we'll sort it out.'

She wailed, 'But we can't. It's Ivor.'

'Have you quarrelled?'

'No, no, you don't understand. He's dead.'

'He's what?'

'Dead, Max.'

'But he was going to drive you home,' Max said, idiotically. He gathered his thoughts. 'What happened? Did he have a heart attack?'

'No. Max, I need you. He's been killed. Please come back. I'm at the hotel.'

'I'm on my way.'

* * *

When Max arrived at the hotel, Stella had left a message at the desk, and a wide-eyed hotel receptionist directed Max to her room.

She was sitting on a chair beside her bed, wearing a dressing gown, accompanied by a female police officer. Her face was almost free of make-up, apart from messy mascara trails under her eyes, from crying.

The police officer stirred milk into a cup as Max entered. 'Mr Ramshore?'

Stella managed to put on a show for the officer. 'My darling Max,' she cried. 'Thank you so much for rushing here to look after me. I don't know what I would do without you.'

The police officer eyed the pair of them, her expression faintly cynical.

'Family liaison officer?' Max queried.

The officer nodded. 'PC Franks,' she said.

'I'm grateful to you,' he said. 'For looking after my ex-wife.' He turned to Stella. 'Tell me what happened.'

She wailed, 'I really don't know. I came out of hospital late yesterday – they made me hang about for hours and hours.' Catching the police officer's glance at Max, she continued more calmly, 'Still, they're very busy, even at weekends. Ivor said I wasn't fit for the drive to Surrey, and we should stay here for a few days. I was pleased because that gave me a chance to see Joe again. And you, of course.' She smiled at PC Franks. 'Max and I have had our ups and downs, but we're always there for each other, when it matters.'

Max ignored the untruth as she went on, between sniffs, 'Then, Ivor had a text on his phone. Or, maybe it was two. I'm not sure. Anyway, he said he had some business to attend to and he wanted to get me some chocolates. He thought I needed cheering up after – you know – my little illness.'

Max wondered how much Stella had revealed of her half-hearted suicide attempt.

'But he didn't come back. I tried his phone after a while, but he didn't answer, and I waited for hours, until at last I – er – I had a small drink, and I was so tired I must have fallen asleep.'

Max frowned. He hated the thought of Stella drinking herself into a stupor, especially so soon after hospital treatment.

'The first thing I heard this morning was this terrible hammering on my hotel door, and it was the police, coming to tell me the – the dreadful news about Ivor. They found him in the woods.'

Max stiffened. 'The woods? You don't mean...'

'Leigh Woods, where you and I met.'

Genuine tears welled in her eyes. Max gave her his handkerchief. While she mopped her face he spoke to the police officer.

'Can you tell me how Mr Wrighton died? I take it there was no accident.'

'I'm sorry, sir. I can't give you any further information,' but the look on the young woman's face told Max what he needed to know.

He asked Stella, 'Do you want to go back to Surrey?'

She shook her head. 'No. I couldn't bear to be there any longer, in that house, without Ivor. Oh dear, there will be all sorts of arrangements to make, with his funeral and so on, although Ivor and I are not – official – in any way. Just friends. Close friends.' She offered Max's handkerchief back to him. 'I have some of Ivor's here.' She opened a drawer beside the bed and took out two beautifully ironed squares, each with a small train embroidered in the corner. 'Oh dear,' she sobbed, 'Poor Ivor. I gave these to him for his birthday. I used to tease him about his name. Ivor, you see, like Ivor the little Welsh engine in the TV programme – Ivor was Welsh, of course,' she explained.

She gave a tremulous smile. 'I think I'll ask Joe if I can stay with him for a few days. That would be best, wouldn't it?'

Max was torn between relief that she didn't want him to take her in, and sympathy for Claire. He made a supreme effort. 'You can stay with me, Stella, if you like. Just until the wedding...'

Stella smiled at the police officer. 'My ex-husband is remarrying soon.' She laid a hand on Max's arm. 'No, I don't want to come between you and your Libby. I'll talk to Joe. I'm sure he'll take pity on his poor old mother.'

22

OMELETTE

Libby bundled Fuzzy into her wicker cat basket, much to the cat's very vocal disgust, and loaded her with her bed – the one she hardly ever used – into the newly repaired Citroen. She added a selection of cat toys, feeding bowls and sachets of cat food; the expensive kind, for Fuzzy would tolerate nothing less. Satisfied Fuzzy had everything she needed, she drove to Max's house.

She arrived just as his car swung into the drive, and followed him to the house. 'I didn't know you were going out,' she said, as they hugged. 'And you look terrible. Is something wrong? By the way, I've brought Fuzzy, so she can get used to your house.'

She bustled around the kitchen, cooking omelettes, as he told her the story.

'Joe came to take his mother home, so I know she's safe, at least, and I rang DCI Morrison. Ivor Wrighton's death didn't take place in his area, but he's working on it, because of the similarities with Carys Evans' murder. He told me that Ivor had almost exactly the same cause of death – hit over the side of the head by a blunt object, possibly a tree branch. Our killer's a creature of habit, it seems. That's all he had so far, except to say that they've checked Ivor Wrighton's phone records for that day. He received a couple of texts, one at around the time he left the hospital. Unfortunately, whoever sent that text used a brand-new pay-as-you-go phone.'

'A burner?' Libby said.

'Exactly. I'm afraid our villains watch as many USA crime series on Netflix as the rest of us. Still, it tells us a little more. Someone contacted Ivor, presumably to entice him into the woods. Must have been someone he knew well – it's December, after all. No one would agree to meet a stranger there at this time of year.'

Max looked uncomfortable. He'd met Stella in the same woods.

Libby concentrated on the new evidence. Ivor's body had been found in the same place as Carys Evans', and he'd been killed in almost exactly the same way, but she knew of no connection between the two victims.

Did Ivor's death have anything to do with his relationship with Stella? Had her stalker turned violent? If so, it was just as well she was staying safely in Somerset, with Joe.

'I'm so sorry about all this,' Max said. 'I'd no idea this business with Stella was going to jump out of the woodwork, just before our wedding, and I didn't take it seriously enough. Stella's always been a drama queen, and I thought she was crying wolf. Thank heaven she's OK.'

'It's not your fault,' Libby said. 'We both come with baggage, don't we? But her man, Ivor, killed – that's shocking. I suppose...' she stopped herself in mid-sentence. Since coming to Exham on Sea, she'd been involved in several murder cases and she was used to talking about the victims in a matter-of-fact way. It was easier to investigate when she felt detached from them. But this murder was very personal to Max. Whatever he felt about his ex-wife, Libby wouldn't say the words that hovered on the tip of her tongue – *Do you think Stella had anything to do with it?*

There was no need. Max took her hands. 'I know what you're thinking. We have to wonder whether Stella's involved, but I can't imagine how. She was in the hotel when he was killed, still recovering from her overdose, although I suppose she could have paid someone to do the dirty work.' He forced a smile. 'But if I know Stella, and she wanted to get rid of someone, she'd be far more likely to feed them poison herself. Arsenic, perhaps, in the sugar bowl. That used to be a thing in the nineteenth century, I believe.' He stabbed at his omelette and forked a tiny square into his mouth. It tasted fine, but his mouth was dry and he couldn't swallow. 'Do you mind if I leave it? No appetite, I'm afraid.'

Libby leaned across the table and squeezed his arm. 'Me neither.'

'I thought,' said Max, 'this was all about Exham, but Ivor's never even been here, so far as I'm aware. Where's the link? I'm convinced there has to be a connection – two murders in almost exactly the same circumstances can't just be coincidence.'

Tired of thinking in circles, Libby let her eyes wander to Fuzzy. On this, her first visit, she'd ventured carefully into every room in the house, sniffing suspiciously in corners and leaping in the air at the slightest sound, as though someone had fired a gun.

Bear was still following her like an anxious mother on a child's first day at preschool, while Shipley danced around them both, having the time of his life, playing a game of doggy chicken. He crept as close to Fuzzy as he could before she retaliated with a flick of her paw, then jumped out of range and waited, tail twitching, until he'd plucked up the courage for another attack.

'Shipley can't understand why Fuzzy's not scared,' Libby said. 'He doesn't realise she's chased more dogs than he's had hot dinners. Or any dinners for that matter. At least she's keeping her claws sheathed.'

'I reckon she'll keep Shipley under control far better than we do,' Max agreed. 'He's so much improved, since his training, but I'm worried he'll slip back into old ways. Can't we use him more when we're investigating?'

'That reminds me. He did one of his stop and point moves, when we were on the Santa Special, but I couldn't understand why. He was pointing at one of the mums.'

Max rubbed his chin, thoughtfully. 'Which one?'

Libby had to search her memory. 'Mrs – um – she had a son called Joseph. Big lady.'

'Atkins? Was that the name? Tired-looking woman?'

'Not surprising she's tired – Joanna told me she has five children. Do you know her? You seem to know everybody.'

'Only people from school, and that was a good few years ago,' Max said. 'Mrs Atkins and her brood have moved into the area since then. I wonder if there's a Mr Atkins? But I digress. The point is, I met her at the vet's surgery, and Shipley played the same game. I thought she might have food in her bag, or something. Anyway, I had to almost drag him away. Isn't it odd? Still, that's less important than these murders.'

'And the emails containing silly nursery rhymes seemed like a joke, at first. Someone poking fun at local people. I don't think it's at all funny, now. Do you?'

Max frowned. 'Carys Evans' death made this a serious business. One of the odd things is the timing. Why send her an email when she was already dead?'

'Maybe the killer was after her anyway, and it just happened that the emails came at around the same time.'

Max scraped the remains of his omelette into the kitchen

compost bin. 'Which takes the emails back to being just a practical joke.'

Libby shook her head. 'I don't buy that any more. Here's another idea – what if Carys' murder was the first event, and then, the killer thought he'd muddy the waters by sending out the nursery rhymes?'

'Bizarre, but possible. A sort of elaborate game?'

'So the killer wanted Carys and Ivor dead. We should concentrate on finding a connection between Carys and Ivor.'

Max pondered for a moment. 'I don't think we can drop the Exham aspect entirely. Those rhymes must mean something, but I agree, events are pointing towards a Carys–Ivor link. We need to know more about both victims. I haven't looked into Maurice Noakes, Carys' son, yet. Stella's phone call put it right out of my head. I'll get on to it tomorrow.'

Libby grinned. 'Maurice is definitely sitting at the top of my list, expecting his mother to leave him a nice nest egg. Then, when the money went to Gladys instead, trashing her shop and demanding the same amount. The circumstantial evidence points to him, but something feels wrong, psychologically. While you're researching Maurice, I think I'll visit Claire. I'd like her professional view as a psychologist on men killing their mothers. If you don't mind me going to see your daughter-in-law?'

Max threw up his hands. 'What's mine is yours – or will be in a couple of weeks. Don't forget Stella's staying with Joe and Claire.'

Libby grinned. She was well aware of that. 'I'd like to meet her.'

'Are you sure about that?' Max peered at her face. 'What are you really up to?'

23

BREAD AND CHEESE

It had seemed such a good idea yesterday, when Libby emailed Claire to see if she was free for lunch. She'd replied:

I can't get away from Hereford, as I have clients in the morning and afternoon, but if you're willing to drive up here I'd love to see you. We can meet at home – Joe's taking his mother out for the day. PS bring Bear.

Heavy black clouds lowered from the sky, threatening rain, or even worse, sleet or snow. 'Don't worry, It never snows in the west country,' Mandy had told her.

'Everyone says that, but it snowed last year.'

'That was an exception. Usually, it only snows deep in the valleys and high on the hills. Some of the villages near Exmoor get snowed in. I'd stay clear of those, if I were you.'

'I won't be going out in the countryside. It's motorways and cities only, this trip.'

Libby encouraged Bear into the Land Rover.

Max had agreed to look after Shipley, still on the lookout for something useful for the spaniel to do.

'Why don't you just enjoy his company, like you do with Bear?' she'd asked.

'I do – but I'm sure he'd be happier using his special skills.'

'Running in circles and racing along the beach, so he can pretend he doesn't hear when we call, you mean?'

Max chuckled, and Libby realised how rarely she was hearing that sound. They used to laugh all the time. Stella's problems were making Max miserable. The sooner they solved the murder mystery and caught the Rhymer, the better. Darkening skies accompanied Libby's drive to Hereford, as the threatened rain drew closer. Was this a mistake? Taking the quicker, motorway route, rather than the pleasant meander along the River Wye she would have preferred, Libby breathed a sigh of relief as she finally parked in the centre of the city, within sight of the beautiful cathedral.

Claire was already waving from the door of the small, terraced house she shared with Joe. 'Quick, before the downpour starts.'

The first drops fell on Libby and Bear as they hurried inside.

The house was like a Tardis, seeming far bigger inside than out. Built way back in the nineteenth century, the rooms were tall and deep, leading back to a small square of garden.

Claire led the way into the kitchen. 'This,' she said, 'is the reason we bought this house – for the Aga. It keeps the whole place warm. Of course, it's almost impossible to cook with and we use the microwave, mostly, but it feels homey, doesn't it?'

A huge quilt hung in pride of place on one wall. Libby couldn't resist examining it closely, while Claire fed Bear biscuits. 'You didn't make this, did you?'

'I did. My mother is from Maine, and she taught me how to

quilt. Joe works such unsocial hours, it helps to have something useful to pass the time.'

'It's just beautiful.'

Claire was busy, so there was no time to waste. They settled at the cosy scrubbed oak table, in the comfortable kitchen, plates of bread, fruit and cheese in front of them, and talked about murder.

'Specifically, sons and mothers. How likely is it that a son would kill his mother in cold blood?'

'If you asked Joe that while Stella's in residence, he'd say it was a miracle his own mother's still breathing. She's driving him up the wall.'

'I'm sorry I missed her. Max is so churned up about her that I'm frantic with curiosity.'

'If I were you, I'd keep away. She's a trouble magnet, with a worrying level of alcohol intake. Joe's taken to marking the level in the gin bottle.'

Claire cut a neat triangle of Somerset Cheddar, balanced it on a slice of the crusty loaf Libby had brought, and topped it with onion chutney as she considered.

'But, to get back to your question about this Maurice killing his mother for money. I think you're right to doubt it. Murdering a mother is one of the last taboos, although it does happen, occasionally. Usually, a matricide, as it's called, happens after a quarrel or as part of a spree in which multiple family members die.'

'Like the Jeremy Bamber case, where both parents, a sister and two nephews all died in their farmhouse?' Libby shivered.

'That's right. There was also a case in 1929, when a man took out a life insurance policy and strangled his mother on the day it matured, but most often, an apparently cold-blooded perpetrator like that turns out to suffer from schizophrenia.'

'What about psychopaths?'

'Well, that's a form of personality disorder, although it wouldn't help to get the villain off in a court of law. It might affect sentencing, and he would likely end up in hospital rather than prison. But, as I say, it's very rare.'

Libby nodded, glad to have her instincts confirmed. 'The sister, Gladys, pointed the finger at the estranged son.'

'Don't take my word as gospel truth, but it would be highly unusual.'

As they finished eating, they chatted over the wedding arrangements, and the news of Sarah's pregnancy. Claire said, 'I thought I'd make a quilt to celebrate your son's baby. Do you think he'd like that?'

'Sarah and Robert would be thrilled to bits. Especially as I'm so hopeless with crafts, I probably won't even manage a pair of bootees for the poor thing.'

Claire showed some drawings, saying in a matter-of-fact voice, 'Since I won't be making one for a child of my own, I'd love to do something for your grandchild.'

Libby hesitated, not wanting to overstep the mark but glad Claire had raised the matter. Secretly, that had been the main reason for Libby's visit. She had been worried by the bleak look on Claire's face as Robert had announced the baby news. 'You won't be having babies? By choice?' Was that tactful enough?

'Not really. Not my choice, anyway, but Joe's against having children. What with his job, and the bad record police officers have with divorce, and his own parents splitting up, not to mention his mother's general lack of stability, he thinks we should stay as we are.'

'But you don't agree?'

Claire chewed on her lip. 'I'm getting older; almost thirty-five.

My clock's ticking. When Robert and Sarah announced their news, I thought I was going to cry.'

Libby threw her hands in the air. 'These men? Why can't they see what's in front of their noses? Have you told Joe how you feel?'

'No. And, please don't say anything, Libby. I know you like to help, and we love you for that, but I need to decide what I really want. How badly do I want children? When I'm sure, I'll talk to Joe, myself.'

That was the nicest way Libby had ever been told to mind her own business. 'I won't interfere,' she agreed. 'Don't worry.'

The storm had increased as she left, rain filling the gutters by the side of the road and drumming on the roof of the car.

'Some problems can't even be solved with cake,' she murmured to Bear, as she turned the windscreen wipers to full and pumped up the heating. 'Let's get home.'

* * *

As Libby drove away, the weather worsened further. It was only just past two o'clock, but it felt like night-time, with the sun entirely obscured by clouds. Hailstones hammered at the window, leaving a carpet of white stones as big as pebbles on the road.

She slowed the car, glad she wasn't driving her little purple Citroen.

Heavier and faster, the stones fell, turning for a few moments of relief into snowflakes.

The hiatus didn't last, and the storm grew stronger, until rain was falling so fast the windscreen wipers couldn't keep up.

Libby, never a very confident driver, wondered whether it was safe to continue. She drew into a service station, along with a host of other vehicles, left the Land Rover and queued for an over-priced coffee.

As the storm grew worse, she made up her mind. The Inn at the station allowed dogs, so rather than fight the weather, she'd buy a toothbrush, text Max, and stay overnight.

24

DING DONG BELL

Next morning, Max yawned and stretched. He'd spent most of last night glued to his computer, and his stomach was rumbling. He'd discovered as much as he could about Maurice Noakes, and it hadn't made happy reading.

Abandoned by his mother, Maurice had lived with his father, Peter, until he left home at the age of sixteen, with no qualifications apart from a GCSE in technology.

He had a police record, beginning with an ASBO banning him from the streets of Swindon, which he'd broken with regularity.

As he grew up, he turned into a regular shop-lifter, eventually spending a few months in prison.

Along with a bunch of friends from that prison sojourn, Maurice had taken part in the armed robbery of a building society in Swindon, driving the getaway vehicle. Apparently accident-prone, he'd managed to run the car and its three passengers straight into a police car speeding towards the crime scene.

As the car had provided overwhelming evidence of guilt, including lavishly finger-printed sawn-off shotguns, a set of balaclava masks, and a bag full of used notes totalling twenty thousand pounds, justice had been swift. Maurice had been banged up for ten years and let out after five.

At least, Max discovered, the man had never been accused of direct violence, although one of his companions had hit an old man with the butt of his gun during the robbery.

After leaving prison, he'd changed jobs and names with regularity, losing contact with both his parents. His father appeared to have written his son off long ago and moved north, where he currently lived with his second wife in Manchester.

Despite the man's criminal record, Max found little to suggest either that Maurice would set out to murder his mother, or that he would have the originality or computing skills to send nursery rhyme emails from untraceable addresses to people he couldn't know. As Max, wrapped in a towel, hair still wet from the shower, was about to head downstairs for the kind of fat-fuelled fried egg, bacon and sausage breakfast Libby wanted him to avoid, Libby rang.

He yawned again as he answered the phone.

'Another late-night session at your desk?' Libby chuckled. 'Did you eat properly?'

'Coffee, mostly. I was planning an enormous breakfast, full of carbs, until you rang – but now I feel guilty.'

'One big breakfast won't hurt. Enjoy yourself. Listen, though, I wanted to tell you something.'

There was a serious note in Libby's voice that set a nerve in Max's cheek twitching. 'What's wrong?'

'Nothing, really, except that I got one of those emails this morning.'

'A rhyme?' Max bit his lip. He shouldn't really feel surprised. The rhymes seemed to be spreading like wildfire.

'*Ding Dong Bell*. Do you know it?'

'I most certainly do. One of the nastiest rhymes my mother sang to me, I always thought.' He murmured,

> 'Ding dong bell
> Pussy's in the well.
> Who put him in?
> Little Johnny Green.
> Who pulled him out?
> Little Johnny Stout.
> What a naughty boy was that
> To try to drown poor pussy cat
> Who ne'er did any harm
> But killed all the mice in the farmer's barn.'

'Wow. I thought you'd need to look it up. Max, I know I'm being silly, but I suppose Fuzzy's all right, is she? You're at home, aren't you?'

'I'm sure she's upstairs, but I'll go and check, and get back to you.'

Max searched in the airing cupboard, under the stairs and in every bedroom, but there was no sign of Fuzzy. Refusing to admit to anxiety, he moved through the downstairs rooms, but still no Fuzzy.

Now, he was worried. What would he tell Libby if her cat had disappeared?

He tried to put himself into Fuzzy's mind. What did a cat think about? Food, mostly, he supposed. Did Fuzzy like to catch her own mice at night? But, she'd been inside while he worked. He'd come back from the kitchen once, to find her stretched out on his keyboard, and he was sure she'd moved to a cosy spot beside the boiler. How could a slightly overweight, marmalade cat have escaped from a house with no cat flap, in the middle of winter when all the windows except the one in Max's bedroom were closed?

Shipley appeared, wet nose thrust into Max's hand, as if in sympathy.

'Where's she gone?' Max asked.

Shipley gazed at him.

'Are you trying to tell me something?'

Shipley shifted his weight, as though about to run.

'Oh, very well. Show me.'

Shipley trotted off, leading the way to Max's study.

'She's not in here. I looked.'

Shipley went into his 'frozen' pose, eyes fixed on the French door.

Max walked across and touched the door with one hand. It moved a little. 'That's odd. I'm sure I locked it last night.' He went outside and examined the door. There was no sign of forced entry. 'Maybe I hadn't locked it and the wind blew it open? Is that how Fuzzy escaped?' he asked Shipley, who'd followed him out. 'Pity you can't speak,' Max muttered.

Back in his study, he stood in the centre of the floor and let his gaze roam over every inch of the room. Peace reigned, and nothing was out of place. Not on the bookshelves, nor on the coffee table where Max liked to rest his feet.

He shuffled the papers on his desk. Nothing seemed to be missing, and the rest of the desk was tidy. The mouse lay further away from the computer than usual, but that meant very little.

'Shipley, no one's been here. I must have left the door on the latch by mistake. I was tired. Now, the question is, where did that cat go, and if she's lost, what do I say to Libby? We'd better get outside again and find her. Wait a minute.' He grabbed the cat bed and held it to Shipley's nose. 'Have a good sniff at that and help me find this cat.'

Shipley followed him through the door, into the garden. Once outside, he quartered the garden, sniffing in circles, nose low to the ground, tail in the air, stopping at intervals to investigate.

Appearing to pick up Fuzzy's scent, he trotted off towards an apple tree at the end of the garden, stopped and barked.

Fuzzy appeared, fur raised in a ruff at her neck, back arched.

Shipley barked again, but Fuzzy stood her ground. The dog wagged his tail.

Fuzzy hissed.

'Leave her alone, boy,' Max advised.

Shipley, instead, moved closer. For a long moment, the two animals faced each other, then Fuzzy leapt in the air, landing inches away from Shipley and dealing him a sharp whack in the face with her paw.

The dog turned tail and ran back into the house.

Max, deciding an angry cat was best left outside, followed Shipley indoors and inspected his nose for scratches. 'No damage done, idiot dog.'

Fuzzy sauntered inside, wandering past Shipley as though he didn't exist. Meekly, Shipley let her pass.

'She's definitely the boss, Ships.'

Relieved, Max sent a text to Libby, telling her all was well with the cat. Then, he sat for a long time at his desk, fingering the mouse and wondering. He'd never left the door unlocked before. Especially in winter.

* * *

Libby, alone in her nondescript hotel room, read Max's text with relief. Fuzzy was safe. Still, she couldn't shake off a mild attack of self-pity. She should have been getting married in a few days, and it didn't seem fair to be stuck half-way up the motorway in a face-less hotel.

'Maybe a spot of retail therapy will help,' she told Bear. 'Bristol has plenty of Christmas market stalls just now, and they're outdoors, so you can come too.' She called Max, wanting to hear his voice again. 'I'm coming home later today, now the weather's cleared, but I thought I'd stop off in Bristol and do some shopping. You know, for the wedding, and Christmas.'

'Christmas?' he'd said, as though he'd never heard of it.

'It's only a few weeks away. I won't even ask if you've done any present shopping.'

The groan on the other end of the phone told her all she needed to know.

'I suppose, as we'll be married by then, you think I should do all the shopping for both of us,' she said.

'Good idea. By the way, I found out plenty about Maurice's background.' Max shared the results of his researches.

She said, 'Claire thinks he's unlikely to have killed his mother, though, psychologically speaking. It hardly ever happens.'

'But, we can't rule him out, yet. He may be the exception that proves the rule.'

Libby's spirits rose as they talked, and by the time she'd checked out of the hotel, she was humming 'We Wish you a Merry Christmas' to herself.

'Come on, Bear. Let's shop until we drop.'

The skies, so grey and sodden yesterday, had gradually cleared, and before long, the sun shone brightly in a blue sky, with hardly a cloud to be seen.

The streets of Bristol were alive. Libby smelled mulled wine, hot dogs and bacon baps, as she threaded her way through the pop-up Christmas stalls. 'It's just as well Shipley isn't here,' she told Bear, as she took a long breath, inhaling the scent of cinnamon, clove and orange. 'These smells would drive him crazy.'

On the corner, a Salvation Army band launched into carols. Libby hummed along to 'The First Noel', 'The Holly and the Ivy', and 'We Three Kings', dropped coins in the collecting bag and wandered from one stall to another, buying gifts for everyone she could think of: a silver necklace for Ali, a jewel-encrusted spider pendant on a purple ribbon for Mandy, and dangly earrings for Sarah. Buying for her pregnant daughter-in-law made her smile. This time next year, she'd be a granny, and with any luck, the baby would visit at Christmas, to crawl around under the Christmas tree and pull Fuzzy's tail.

She spent a long time choosing baby clothes.

'Is it for a boy or a girl?' asked the stallholder.

'I've no idea, yet, but I want things that are cheerful, in green or yellow, not pastel pink or blue.'

The stallholder smiled. 'These are from Brazil. They like bright colours over there, where the sun shines and they dance the samba.'

'Perfect.'

Speaking of Brazil reminded Libby of Ali. She'd need a new dress for the wedding, and she probably wouldn't bring anything special with her, so Libby searched through the stalls for velvet dresses. Ali would love something vintage.

As Libby flicked through a rail of twenties and thirties clothes, a low growl from Bear stopped her in her tracks. 'What's the matter?'

He growled again. Libby could see nothing nearby that was likely to upset him, but he pulled on the lead, tugging her away from the stall.

'Sorry,' she murmured. 'I'll have to come back later. My dog has a mind of his own.'

She gazed into the crowd, expecting to see a familiar face among the shoppers milling around. She couldn't imagine who'd have that effect on Bear. Who had the friendly animal ever disliked? He loved everybody, except when they attacked Libby or one of her friends.

She scrutinised nearby faces, all red-nosed and pink-cheeked from the cold air, their heads insulated by woolly hats. She saw nobody she knew, and Bear had relaxed. It must have been a false alarm. Perhaps it was his rheumatism making him grumpy. If that was the case, he needed to get somewhere warm as soon as possible.

The shopping trip had lost its charm. 'Come on, Bear, let's get back to the car and drive home.'

25

COTTAGE

When Libby wanted to think, she often turned to baking. There was something so comforting about beating eggs and sugar together, even when her industrial-grade mixer did the work.

Back at the cottage, she ran a finger along a shelf crammed with ingredients; vanilla, elderflower cordial... It made her mouth water just to look at them.

As she tasted, discarded, and tasted again, her mind roamed freely over the events in Exham and Bristol. She was worried about Max. She'd learned to lean heavily on his unflappable good sense, but just now he was anxious and distracted – not surprising, given Stella's attention-grabbing fake suicide attempt, swiftly followed by the death of her latest man friend.

Her phone rang. Angela, keen to talk about the imminent opening of the café, could hardly restrain her enthusiasm. 'The trouble is, Libby, it's so cold in the shop, I think my nose is about to drop off. Could I come round and chat?'

The doorbell rang before Libby had done more than wash her hands.

But it wasn't Angela on the doorstep.

'Ali?'

Libby dropped the towel she was using to wipe cake mixture from her arms and enveloped her daughter in a hug. She'd been longing for this moment for so many months, and had begun to doubt Ali would ever come home.

'Hi, Mum. I'm pleased to see you, too, but can I come in? It's freezing out here.'

Libby choked back tears. 'What are you doing here?' she asked, stupidly. 'You're not due for more than a week.'

Ali laughed, a sound Libby had missed so much. 'I got a place on an earlier flight. But I have a lot to tell you. Shall I put the kettle on?'

'Just let me look at you for a moment. Sit down. I'll make the tea. You look tired – the journey, I expect. What do you want to eat? Oh,' she remembered, 'Angela will be here in a moment.'

'Angela? Oh, yes, your friend. The one who's going to manage the café while you work part-time, solve mysteries and play at being in the police service.'

Libby opened cupboards, pulled out cake tins and coffee, grabbed mugs from a shelf. 'How do you know all that? I'm sure I haven't told you.'

'No. Your emails are full of dogs, beaches and cake recipes. Fortunately, I have Robert as my spy, and he's been telling me what you really get up to. He also regales me with long diatribes about our ancestors, who used to live around here. One was a maid in some stately home, he says.'

'Oh yes. I'm hoping he'll join the Exham History Society – we could do with some young input. In fact—'

Ali held up her hand. 'No,' she said, firmly. 'I'm not staying here for long. Just your wedding, and Christmas. Not nearly long enough to get involved in Exham life.'

Libby hid her disappointment. She'd been hoping Ali was back for good.

Ali chortled. 'I know exactly what you're thinking. You don't have much of a poker face, Mum.'

'That's what Max says.'

'Ah, yes. Your enigmatic fiancé. I only met him once, before I left, but I knew there was something brewing between the two of you.'

'You couldn't possibly know,' Libby objected. 'We were just friends, then.'

'As I said – absolutely no poker face. Solved any juicy murders lately?'

Before Libby could tell her about the nursery rhyme emails, Angela arrived.

Libby looked on like a proud mother hen as Ali, no longer the petulant teenager who'd walked away from university on a whim, talked to Angela with exactly the right mix of warmth and respect.

As she watched, Libby began to wonder if all was well. Ali had lost weight. Her eyes were large and dark in a pale, almost translucent face. Surely someone who'd lived in the heat of Brazil, currently enjoying a scorching summer, should have some colour in her cheeks?

Angela refused to sit. 'I'm not going to stay. You two must have a lot to talk about. I just wanted to show you the material for the last of the soft furnishings. I'll leave it with you and catch up later.'

Despite Libby's entreaties, she left, promising to return tomorrow to discuss the arrangements for opening the café.

'Can I help with that?' Ali asked.

'You bet. All hands to the pump.'

Left alone with Ali, Libby hesitated. Should she mention the weight loss?

She opened her mouth and closed it again in silence. Claire had asked her to mind her own business. Like her, Ali was an adult. If she had something to tell her mother, she would choose her own moment, and if not, a few weeks of home-cooked food would fatten her up nicely. Libby began to plan menus in her head.

Bear, bored by proceedings, snored gently in the corner of the sitting room.

'Now,' Ali said, as they sorted through cheerful nautical striped cushion fabric and seagull-inspired tablecloths, 'what's going on? I feel dreadful about making you delay the wedding, and Robert said Max is furious.'

'Did he? No, I don't think so. Max was fine about it.'

'Well, I wouldn't blame him. But I couldn't really help it. You see, Andy, that I went with – you remember Andy?'

Libby had met him briefly, as he whisked Ali away, giving Libby less than a day's notice. She remembered a tall young man with curly hair and an air of good sense.

'Well, Andy and I have been an item ever since we went away. You'll like him, I promise. He's a doctor – I think I told you, and – well, the fact is, I love him, and I love my work out there.' She grinned, looking into Libby's face, as though checking how her mother was taking the news. 'Well, to cut a long story short, I'm going to be a doctor too. I have a university place out there.'

'In Brazil?' Libby bit her lips, determined not to fuss.

'My interview clashed with the flight I'd planned. But I got a place on the course and I start in the New Year.'

Libby closed her eyes for a moment, trying to take in this sudden news. 'Seriously. A doctor? In Brazil? Why not in England? Isn't it expensive?'

'Don't start worrying, Mum. Just break out the champagne. Andy's going to help pay for it. It's all settled. I'll work part-time, as well. I really mean it, Mum. I'm not going to give up, this time. And, by the way, I'm staying with Robert and Sarah while I'm here, so you don't need to run around getting my room ready, or moving Mandy, or making any of those arrangements you're planning.'

While Libby, stunned and excited, searched for words, Ali ended with a grin.

'One more thing. If you think you're having a quiet wedding, you're out of luck. Robert says half of Exham is planning to be there, so you'd better be looking your best.'

26

THREATS

In Hope Cottage next morning, Libby scrolled down the list of names in her inbox. There were several messages from Angela, dealing with plans for the café opening and a silly, fond message from Max. Her happy smile froze on her face. What was this? A message from an unknown sender.

Her heartbeat sped up. Another nursery rhyme?

She clicked on the email.

You think you're clever, don't you? Running around town, interfering in our business? Well, we're watching you. Better take care. Nice dogs by the way. Especially that big one – wouldn't want anything to happen to him, would we? Maybe keep your nose out of things that don't concern you. See you soon.

Libby filled her lungs as full as they would go, before letting her breath out slowly, trying to calm the churning in her stomach.

This was worse than the nursery rhymes.

Far more scary.

So far, the police had paid little attention to the anonymous emails, but Libby was sure they'd take this seriously.

Time to speak to DC Gemma Humberstone.

* * *

Gemma agreed to call in to the bakery on her way to visit some local teenagers who'd been reported for scratching keys along car doors in town.

'Can't stay long,' Gemma said, as she and PC Tim Green pushed open the bakery door.

Mandy, sharing the morning shift, grinned. 'The first rush is over, but we'll be busy in a few minutes. Here, Constable, try one of these.' She offered him one of the misshapes they kept in the kitchen. 'I hope you'll be coming to the café opening?'

PC Green blushed and stammered. Libby would have a word with Mandy later. It wasn't fair to lead the poor lad on while she and Steve were an item.

She took Gemma to one side and showed her a printout of the email. 'We also suspect someone's been sneaking around the house. The cat escaped from Max's house yesterday and he's sure he'd locked all the doors.'

'Not much to go on. We only go out to burglaries when we think the villain's still there. Police shortages, you know.' She read the email again. 'I can't do much about this, either, Libby. It's just an empty threat. No place or time, and no reference to hurting you or anyone else. The only real threat is to Bear. But I'll ask DCI Morrison to send a car round from time to time, keep an eye on your cottage and on Max's place. I'm afraid that's the best we can do. We'll have to leave this to you. Keep a lookout for anything odd, and let us know.'

She left, PC Green throwing a last look over his shoulder at Mandy.

'Cheer up, Mrs F,' Mandy said, as the first of the estate agents arrived for their sandwiches. 'Things aren't so bad. The café will be opening in a couple of days, your daughter's arrived in plenty of time for your wedding, and you're going to be a granny. What could be better?'

* * *

'I know Mandy's right. I'm incredibly lucky and I have so much to look forward to, but I can't get rid of a dreadful feeling of foreboding, as though something awful is about to happen.'

Libby was in Angela's house, with her friend and Owen, the new owner of the café and Angela's 'significant other'. As Angela had said, 'boyfriend sounds ridiculous after forty, and man friend makes him sound like a predator.'

'Just call me "your man",' Owen had suggested. 'It makes me feel tall and imposing. Which, as you can see, I am not.'

Libby was surprised how soon she'd learned to feel at ease with Owen. 'I,' she'd said, 'shall call you "Boss" once the café's open.'

'We need to get to the bottom of these spiteful emails, before you allow them to ruin your wedding,' Angela put in. 'Otherwise, we'll have you postponing again, and I want to wear my new dress. Besides, Max might run out of patience.'

Libby's head jerked up. 'Do you think so? I thought he took it very well when I suggested we wait until Ali could be there, but Robert thinks he was furious.'

'Too kind to upset you. Typical Max. Has Ali given you a sensible reason for the delay?'

Libby bit her lip. 'That's one of the things on my mind. She said it clashed with her interview. But she doesn't look too well. I think she's been on some kind of silly diet.'

'Fitting into a dress for the wedding?' Angela suggested.

Libby shook her head. 'As I thought, she hasn't brought one. But I found the perfect dress for her – velvet, dark blue – she'll look like a queen. If it's not too big. Still, Ali's good with a needle.' The thought of Ali at her wedding brought a smile to her face. 'Now, how are we going to find the person sending these emails? Max has been searching for clues online, but whoever's doing it is hiding their identity perfectly. There are no clues at all. In any case, Max is quite distracted over his ex-wife. She's managed to shove an oar right into our wedding plans.'

Owen said, 'Leaving a vengeful ex-wife aside for the moment, do you know of any likely culprits in Exham? Anyone with a grudge against you or any of the others, Libby? Especially you – that last email went a step further than a nursery rhyme.'

'I've racked my brains, trying to think, but I haven't come up with a suitable suspect, so far.'

Angela said, 'What about people you've annoyed, since you've been a private investigator. Like that Chesterton Wendlebury, from the board of Pritchards. He went to prison because of Forest and Ramshore.'

Libby shook her head. 'He's still there. Can't be him. The prison authorities will limit his computer access.'

'Or that other businessman – Terence Marchant? He wanted to set up in competition with you and Frank.'

Owen joined in, 'I bought his premises and interest in the café for a fair price, and it was a business deal. I can't imagine why he'd be upset. It wasn't personal, like the emails.'

Libby looked from Angela to Owen, but they both shook their heads. She sighed. 'We're no further forward, are we? Let's forget the emails for a while, never mind the murders, and talk about the café.'

At least those plans were moving forward smoothly.

Angela said, 'We're giving ourselves time to bed in – make mistakes that won't matter, before the visitors descend at Easter. I haven't run a café before, so I need the practice. Are you ready to supply the cakes?'

Libby grinned. 'That's something I can do standing on my head, and it'll take my mind off these emails. Here are the new recipes...'

With talk of recipes, the pitfalls of baking on new equipment, and the best way to display the chocolates that would take pride of place in the café window, Libby almost forgot there may be someone watching her, someone who bore her some kind of grudge, who'd threatened her and the people – and animals – she loved.

Angela had organised a special meeting of the History Society for Quentin Dobson's talk. Libby was glad of the chance to fill another day. The time before her wedding seemed to drag, painfully slowly, even though she tried to fill her days with phone calls, checking and re-checking the arrangements for the big day, testing cake recipes for the café opening, and wrapping Christmas presents.

'This,' she announced, as Angela's room filled with society members, 'is one of the recipes for the opening of the café on Tuesday.' She carried in a three-layer lemon-iced cake, scattered with carefully preserved summer flowers, 'I'm trusting everyone here will be coming along.'

Jemima Bakewell licked her lips. 'Wouldn't miss it for the world,' she enthused. 'I'm so grateful to you all for letting me come to these meetings, even though I don't live in Exham. Maybe I should move here?'

'You'd be very welcome,' said Margery. Margery much preferred older members of the society. Their presence helped her to keep a distance between her husband and Annabel

Pearson.

Jemima beamed with delight at Quentin Dobson's arrival, as their guest speaker. 'I can't wait to talk to you about your fossils,' she gushed.

Libby and Angela shared a smile. Annabel wasn't the only single lady at these meetings.

Quentin Dobson delved into his briefcase and brought out several fossil samples, launching into a long explanation of the Jurassic era, its flora and fauna, as faces glazed over.

Libby used the distraction to take a good look at the society members in the room. Could any of these people be the Rhymer?

Jemima Bakewell, her eyes fixed on Quentin's face, followed his every word with bated breath, nodding along as he spoke.

Annabel Pearson sat quietly in the corner, beautifully made-up, pretending not to notice the glances sent her way by Archie Phillips, the Wells Cathedral librarian.

When Quentin Dobson stopped talking, Libby had hardly heard a word. She soon realised she wasn't alone. Everyone, it seemed, was far more interested in the email epidemic.

Annabel said, 'I haven't had any more nursery rhyme poison-pen emails. Has anyone else?'

Quentin's angular face was alight with interest. 'Poison pen, did you say? How very interesting. It reminds me of that spate of poison-pen letters in Exham, years ago.'

All heads swung his way.

'You mean, this has happened before?' Libby asked.

'Oh, yes. Quite some time ago, now. Before most of you were born. The late sixties, you see. Not everything was peace and love, despite the Beatles.' He chuckled. 'Of course, in those days, the letters were real. Typed, I seem to remember, and sent by post. Snail mail, they'd call it, these days.'

Libby heard Angela give a small gasp. 'I remember something, now you mention it. Not nursery rhymes, but a few letters telling tales about people. Mostly, they were gossip, accusing folk of having affairs. I didn't really notice it, as I wasn't old enough. Still at infant school.'

'Indeed,' Quentin, a little irritated, regained the centre of attention. 'I received one, myself.'

'No!' Joanna had let out the exclamation. She clapped a hand over her mouth. 'I mean...'

'You mean, you can't imagine me being accused of having affairs? Let me tell you, young lady, I was quite the man about town in my day.'

Annabel's face turned red with suppressed laughter. 'Mr Dobson, the big question is, who was sending the letters?'

'The culprit?'

'Yes.'

A hush fell on the room.

Quentin let it draw out, as though he were about to announce the winner of MasterChef.

'It's still a mystery, I'm afraid.' The twinkle in Quentin's eye told Libby he was thoroughly enjoying himself. 'The police tried to find him – or her – but no one knows for certain, to this day.'

They were no farther forward, then. Libby felt deflated. For a moment, it had seemed they were getting close to a breakthrough. She wondered if Max had heard of the letters from the sixties.

Meanwhile, Quentin Dobson was keen to hear about the recent emails.

Annabel said, 'There was mine, the Queen of Hearts, and Joanna's Jack and the Beanstalk.'

Joanna interrupted. 'Mandy had one about her Goth clothes – Little Red Riding Hood.'

Libby joined in, 'I had Ding Dong Bell, and one went to Max –

Baa Baa Black Sheep – and one to an old friend of his, Ollie Redditch. Little Boy Blue, I believe. But the first one had gone to Carys Evans – Lucy Locket. To be honest, they'd be more amusing than scary – except...'

'Except that Carys died.' Quentin was nodding. 'Not so funny, now, is it? And I believe there was another murder at the same spot. Someone completely unconnected to Exham.'

Libby was thinking. 'Ivor Wrighton, the man who was killed, lived with Stella, Max's ex-wife, and someone sent her a rhyme as well. Goosey Goosey Gander.'

She felt a blush rising to her cheeks, and hoped no one had noticed, for she'd suddenly worked out the connection that had been staring her in the face for days.

* * *

'This has all happened before,' Libby finished explaining Quentin Dobson's startling information to Max, later that evening. 'And the police were involved.'

Max whistled. 'They'll have records, then. A pity it's too late to find anything today. But I'll contact DCI Morrison. This opens up a whole new area of investigation.'

'It seems we have a copycat criminal.' Libby mulled this over for a few minutes. 'But the thing that hit me between the eyes was the connection. It's you, Max. You're the one. The only person who connects the Exham on Sea community and Ivor Wrighton, through Stella.'

'That's crazy...' Max stopped in mid-sentence, frowning.

Libby said, 'So, you could be next.'

'Nonsense. Why would anyone want to kill me?'

'Look, if you think of the rhymes as a smokescreen, designed to hide the killer's real intentions, it makes sense. Although, why

he'd want to go to all the trouble of playing complicated games, I
can't imagine. Why not just lure you into the woods, and whack
you on the head? It's worked twice.'

Max was shaking his head. 'I can't see anything like a motive.
And, no one's made any attempt to harm me.'

'But the other day? When your door was unlocked? Do you
think someone had got into the house?' Libby felt sick. The more
she considered the possibility that Max was some kind of target,
the more likely it seemed. 'You have to be careful. Could you ask
Morrison for protection?'

Max laughed. 'You're worrying too much. I'll keep my eyes
open, and I'll cut out the woodland walks for a while.'

'That's not funny.' Libby's voice wobbled.

Max pulled her to him. 'I know, love, and I promise to take it
seriously. In any case, the best solution is to find the Rhymer,
whatever his – or her – twisted reasoning may be. And, you know,
I bet there were newspaper articles about the poison-pen letters
in the sixties. If we could find some of those, they may give us a
clue.'

He settled to work at his desk, while Libby, determined to find
something positive to do, made lists of townspeople she knew
who were around in the sixties.

'Not many,' she muttered. 'Margery and William Halfstead?'

Max said, 'Unlikely. And they wouldn't want to upset you by
getting rid of me. They credit you with saving their marriage,
when Margery thought William was straying. Besides, you told
me they didn't remember anything about the letters.'

'Or so they said. I don't trust anyone at the moment.' She
thought aloud. 'There's Quentin himself, of course, and Amy
Fisher, the vicar. She's probably old enough to remember the
poison pens.'

'Some people may have heard about it from their parents,'

Max pointed out. 'That would add quite a few to the list. Everyone in the area seems to be related, either through birth or marriage.'

They worked in silence for a few minutes, until Max waved an arm to attract her attention.

'Listen to this.'

Libby squinted across the room, refocusing her eyes.

He beckoned. 'As we thought, it's all in the local paper. Watchet seems to have been the centre of the outbreak, where all the letters originated.'

Libby came to his side.

He sniffed the air. 'You smell nice. Are you wearing something special?'

She named a perfume.

He shrugged. 'Never heard of it,' but made a mental note to buy her some for Christmas. Pleased with his subterfuge, he pointed to the screen. 'See? It's the *West Somerset Gazette*, an independent local paper serving that part of Somerset. It loves local scandal, and it has page after page on the poison pen affair. Look.' He read out the article. 'Local MP, Sir Bartholomew Higgs, admitted yesterday that he'd received one of the scandalous anonymous letters circulating in the area. Sir Barnaby was unwilling to share the letter with this newspaper, but said in a statement, *As the letter refers to innocent people, I shall not divulge its contents, but rest assured there is no truth whatsoever in its accusations. I have passed the letter to the police, and confidently expect that the culprit will be found and brought to justice.* Why are you laughing?'

Libby scoffed. 'Innocent people? No truth whatsoever? I bet he was having an extramarital affair. But there's no nursery rhyme. What a pity.'

'Good point.' Max said.

'You sound as though you're thinking.'

'Well, I do sometimes.' He tried to sound hurt. 'But I was wondering, too, why nursery rhymes? What do nursery rhymes mean to people?'

'Childhood? Fun?'

He shook his head. 'There are much darker aspects to them. Many of them date back hundreds of years and refer to disasters. You know, Ring a Ring o' Roses is supposed to be about sneezing as the first sign of the Black Death. We've been looking at the way the rhymes apply to the recipient – the Queen of Hearts, for instance, for a flirt, and Lucy Locket as a suggestion of someone with – ah – loose morals.'

'There's another thing.' Her cheeks were pink.

'Yes,' Max encouraged. 'A brainwave?'

'We've been assuming all the email recipients are victims. But, what if one of them was actually sending to all the others, and sent one to themselves to cover their tracks?'

He grinned at her. 'I love it when you have ideas,' he said.

Libby forced herself to smile. 'I want this sorted before the wedding. I'm not going to marry you if someone's going to bump you off immediately after the ceremony.'

'I'll take care. Now, didn't you tell me you were spending the next few days baking? You need to get those cakes finished before the café opening, keeping one of the best for me, by the way. I'll sit safely at home with the dogs, and keep searching online. Maybe I'll find something in your list of likely recipients of the sixties poison-pen letters.'

Libby slipped her hand behind his neck. 'You can't wait to spend a few hours alone with your PC, can you? Don't worry, I'll leave the two of you alone together. Plus the dogs, for safety. But let's give up, for tonight, and have a nightcap.'

TOASTED CHEESE AND ONION

On Sunday morning, Libby planned to devote the morning to baking for Tuesday's grand opening. As she wrestled with packs of butter that she'd forgotten to leave out of the fridge to soften, Max called. 'The people on your list who admitted to receiving letters back then are long gone from Exham, or have died, and only a few remain in the area. There's a Jane Atkins. She died a few years ago, but there are several of her descendants living nearby, including Mary Atkins, the tired woman with five children I saw at the vet's surgery. There's an Ann Stewart – don't know her at all – and Quentin Dobson. He's still here, of course.'

Max sighed. 'The trouble is, I could spend hours going through information on the last poison-pen event all those years ago, instead of looking into Ivor and Carys' backgrounds—' He broke off.

'What is it?' Libby asked.

'It could be nothing, but it just struck me that Carys and Ivor are both Welsh names.'

'That's true.' Where was Max going with this?

'Stella told me that Ivor was very proud of his Welshness. He even had handkerchiefs with Ivor the Engine on – from the story about the little Welsh train?'

'I remember it. But, why does it matter that Ivor was Welsh?'

'Don't laugh – it's a very long shot – but what if Ivor and Carys knew each other? Could there be a connection? Even a family link? Wales is a small place.'

Libby thought about it. 'It's worth considering. How can we find out? Wait, don't tell me. You'll look it up on the internet. Or...'

'Have you had an idea?'

'I have, and it's brilliant. Instead of you slogging through all this information while I bake cakes, why don't we get an expert on the job?'

'Quentin, you mean?'

'I was thinking of someone closer to home. Robert. He's always asking about our investigations, and he's crazy about old family trees; he spends hours poring over ours. I think we should ask him about the people affected by the original poison-pen letters, and any family they may have, and I'll get him to add Carys into the mix. If she's related to Ivor, he'll find it out. He's like a dog with a bone when he's researching genealogy. It's a long shot, as you say, but it may give us a clue. I'll ring him, now.'

* * *

Robert could hardly wait to get started. 'I'll have some family trees for you in a couple of days,' he promised. 'By the way, have you talked to Ali, yet?'

'What?' Libby's throat tightened at the odd note in his voice. 'What do you mean? Of course I've talked to her. Is there something wrong?'

She heard him mutter.

'Robert. What are you saying?'

'Nothing. I don't know. I mean, she just looks a bit peaky, to me. Sarah thinks so, too.'

That was true. Libby had thought it as soon as she saw her. 'I expect she's tired.'

'Maybe. What would I know? Sarah says I'm hopeless at psychology. Let me get on to these names.'

Libby's mind was only half engaged. Worry over possible danger to Max had distracted her from thinking about Ali's pale face. She'd put her daughter's new aura of calm and quiet down to growing up and working with people with terrible lives of poverty and illness. What if there was another reason, and something was wrong?'

'She's coming to try on her dress today,' she told Robert. 'I'll see if anything's wrong.'

* * *

Ali arrived for her dress fitting at lunchtime. She hadn't yet worn the velvet dress Libby had bought in the market. 'I hope it's not too big,' Libby had said on the phone, biting back the urge to say, 'you've lost weight.'

Ali's cheeks were a little pinker than when she'd arrived, and she tucked into a plate of toasted cheese and onion sandwiches as though she hadn't eaten for a week, but she still looked peaky.

'Shall I make more?' Libby asked, as her daughter finished the last sandwich in two bites.

'No thanks, but I'll try some of that sultana bran loaf.'

'It was always your favourite, when you were at school. What do you eat in Brazil?'

'Plenty of vegetarian food – beans, and rice, and some glorious sun-dried beef when I feel like eating meat. Plus, desserts and sweets made with dulce de leche. Full of calories, of course, but they taste wonderful.'

Libby bit her tongue. At least Ali wasn't starving herself. So, why the weight loss?

Upstairs, Ali slipped into the dress, spinning in front of a mirror, and Libby caught her breath.

'Beautiful,' she said, her eyes misty. 'Just needs a bit of a tuck around the waist.'

'I can fix that,' Ali grinned. 'Easy. What about you. Come on, try on your wedding dress. You're allowed to show me. It's just the groom who mustn't see it before the wedding.'

Obediently, Libby unwrapped the dress that she'd bought weeks ago, but today, her mind wasn't on the wedding.

As she struggled to find the words to ask what was wrong, Ali saved her the trouble. 'Why don't you say it?'

'It?'

'You've been dying to ask. That interview story didn't fool you for a moment, did it?'

'I've known you for too long. But, if you're ready to tell me, I want to hear the truth. Why couldn't you get home in time?'

To Libby's horror, Ali sank onto the bed and burst into tears, grabbing a tissue from the box beside the bed and scrubbing at her eyes. 'I wanted to tell you. You see, Andy and I – well, I expect you know, we've been together ever since we went overseas, I was – I mean, we were thinking about getting married, but we didn't get around to it, and then – then – I found I was pregnant.' She wept harder, and Libby could hardly make out what she was saying. 'And I was going to tell you, when I got to twelve weeks, but it didn't last that long. I had a miscarriage.'

Libby closed her eyes. She'd known something was wrong, but she hadn't begun to guess the truth. If only she'd been there, with Ali. It broke her heart to think of her daughter going through such a terrible event, thousands of miles away. 'Were you in hospital?'

Ali nodded. 'Everyone was very kind, especially Andy, but I wanted you, Mum.'

They clung together, Ali sobbing into her mother's shoulder, as she'd done when she was a child.

When the storm of tears was done, they both wiped their eyes. 'Oh, Ali. I'm so sorry. If only I'd been there.'

'Don't. You'll set me off again. I wanted the baby, even though it meant I might not be able to do the medical qualification. And I wanted to tell you. It was going to be a sort of wedding present. But it all went wrong.'

'You should have told me, Ali. That's what parents are for.'

'I didn't want to spoil things for you. You've been so happy, ever since you met Max. You've been different – setting up your chocolate business, and becoming a private investigator. I'm very proud of you, Mum.'

Libby eyes filled again. 'Stop it,' she warned. 'You'll start me off again and make our dresses wet.'

Ali stood up. 'We should have changed before I dropped the bombshell,' she said. 'Sorry about that.'

'No harm done. We can steam out the creases. And, to be honest, I'm not sure that cream lace dress is right for me. I'm having second thoughts. There's still time to buy something different.'

They took off their outfits, hanging them carefully in poly-thene bags. 'Not very eco-friendly,' Ali pointed out, with a watery smile.

'What are you and Andy going to do now?' Libby asked.

'I don't know, I told him I needed time to think. I wanted to talk to you. You see, the medical training is real. I can do it in Brazil, or come home, if I can get a place in a UK University.'

Libby's heart gave a tiny flip. If only Ali would come back to study in England.

'And Andy?'

'He's said he'll do whatever I want. He's the nicest, most easy-going person, Mum. You'll love him when you get to know him.'

'I'm sure I will.' Libby wasn't sure at all. She'd have to make an effort to forgive him for whisking her daughter so far away, to the other side of the world.

'I wouldn't let him come for the wedding. I wanted to talk to you alone about the future. I know the way I left home was – well, Andy said I was unfair to you.'

'Did he?' That was something.

'He can come for a couple of weeks in the New Year, if you like. You and Robert – and Max – can get to know him.'

On Monday morning, the day before the grand opening, Libby and Mandy were up to their elbows in cake mixture and chocolate, in final preparation for the great day.

'I'm going to miss you, Mrs F, when you're married and living at Max's place.'

'Really? Why?'

'Breakfast, mostly. I can't be bothered with cooking in the morning, but I do like your scrambled eggs. What's that stuff you put on them?'

'Paprika.' Libby added eggs to her mixer and switched it on, the noise prohibiting further chat. She smiled to herself. Mandy was still young, and refused to ditch the Goth clothes or the weird, angular hairstyles, but underneath all that she was delightfully uncomplicated, unlike Ali. Luckily, the two girls got on well together, despite Ali being a few years older.

Libby switched off the motor, and silence descended.

Mandy, filling chocolate cases on the other side of the kitchen, hummed to herself. 'Will you miss the cottage?'

Libby let her gaze roam over the shining surfaces,

hygienic enough to please the most fastidious of inspectors. She'd be working in the kitchen at the café, soon. She'd been tempted to set up another professional-standard kitchen in Max's house, and had pored over catalogues for days, before making her decision. She'd keep her professional baking and chocolate-making life separate from the time she spent with Max.

The café kitchen would be bigger and better.

She'd always be fond of the cottage, though. She'd earned her independence here. In the kitchen, Mandy and she had fought off a killer with a knife, and in the hall, Bear had saved them from an attack by Mandy's father, Bert, in a drunken fury.

Then, she thought of Max, his glasses pushed up on top of his head as he squinted at books, torn between his long-term short-sightedness and his age-related long sight, complaining that his arms weren't long enough, these days. She couldn't wait to share the rest of her life with him.

'It's been fun, living here with you,' she admitted. 'But I can't wait to be married, living with Max and the dogs...'

Mandy grinned. 'You'll miss my music.'

Libby winced. Catatonia was not her style. She said, 'I'm glad you'll still be living here, and I'll see you often at the café.' She lined up a row of tins ready to add the cake mixture. 'How's your mum, by the way?' she asked. Elaine had moved away from Exham after Bert's attack.

'She's still sharing my aunt's place in Bristol. I'm surprised, because she used to bad-mouth Aunt Celia all the time. Her younger sister, you see. She said Celia was always the favourite daughter.'

Libby laughed. 'I never had brothers or sisters, but I would have loved growing up with a sister. Clothes shopping, and gossip, and giggling over boys. I envy big families, even the ones full of step-brothers and -sisters. I can never understand why they quarrel.'

'Talking of quarrelling, how are Fuzzy and the dogs getting along together in that big house?'

Libby recounted how Fuzzy had put Shipley in his place. 'Poor Shipley. He's right at the bottom of the pecking order. He's such a funny creature. He needs a goal in life.'

'That reminds me,' Mandy said. 'I told Steve about your time on the train, and how Shipley behaved so oddly around Mrs Atkins, and he had an idea. He said, some dogs can sniff out illnesses.'

'What sort of illnesses?' Libby was intrigued.

'Well, Parkinson's disease, for one thing, and cancers.'

Libby stopped tasting lemon fillings. 'Oh, my goodness me. Neither Max nor I thought of that, but it's obvious, isn't it? You could be right – Mrs Atkins looked exhausted when I saw her, but I just put that down to tiredness. She has five children.'

'What are you doing?' Mandy said, as Libby dropped spatulas and bowls into the dishwasher.

'I'm going over there, right now.'

'Do you even know where she lives?'

'I don't, but someone at the doctor's surgery will know.'

* * *

Sure enough, when Libby called in at the doctor's surgery, the receptionist admitted to having the addresses of everyone on the doctors' lists – which included pretty much everyone in Exham. But she wouldn't divulge the information. 'I'm sorry, Mrs Forest. It's a doctor – patient confidentiality thing, and more than my job's worth. Why do you need to see her?'

'Oh, just something about our dogs. Shipley's taken a shine to

Mrs Atkins.'

'Then, maybe you should try the vet. They probably don't have to reach the same standards we have to meet in the surgery.'

Marvelling at this instance of professional snobbery, Libby loaded Bear up into the Citroen. 'This could be your last trip in this car,' she told him. 'If the one Alan's found for me is as great as he promises, we'll be saying *au revoir* to this French *voiture*.'

Bear, overflowing the back seat as he always did, grunted companionably.

The vet's surgery was almost empty, the last basket of guinea pigs leaving in the arms of a pink-faced teenager as she arrived.

'Libby. Come in, I'll put the kettle on.' Tanya was an old friend. 'What can I do for you? Bear's looking in fine fettle.'

'Those tablets seem to work. So long as we don't walk too far, he's fine.'

'He'll be fit to follow you down the aisle, then?'

Libby grinned. 'No aisle. It's a register office wedding.'

'What a shame.'

Libby flinched. Why did it matter where she and Max married? Changing the subject, she explained Mandy and Steve's theory about Shipley's ability to spot human illnesses. 'And I need to talk to Mrs Atkins. Do you know where she lives?'

'I can do better than that. Look.' Tanya pointed. Mrs Atkins, three of her troupe of children in tow, was just passing the window.

Libby leapt to her feet, and with barely a thank you, dragged Bear from Tanya's office and out into the street.

Mrs Atkins was shepherding her brood into the library.

Libby followed her inside, leaving Bear tied to a bicycle stand. 'Two minutes, Bear, I promise.'

Breathless, she burbled at Mrs Atkins, her voice low. The last thing she wanted was to frighten the children. However, they were too busy squabbling over the last *How to Train Your Dragon* book on the shelves to overhear.

It sounded ridiculous, when Libby put her suspicions into words.

'Nonsense,' Mrs Atkins said. 'Nothing wrong with me. You'd be tired if you had to chase after these kids all day.' Close up, her skin had an unhealthy, greyish tone. Her cheekbones stood out sharply. 'Maybe you need to train your dog more carefully. That Shipley's a menace, sniffing around people. That's why I won't have a dog in the house.'

'But he has an incredibly good sense of smell.'

'Well, thank you very much.' Mrs Atkins, offended, seemed to grow an inch taller. 'How dare you...'

'Please, just visit the doctor. Check it out?'

'I'll thank you to mind your own business.' Outraged, Mrs Atkins turned her back on Libby and joined her children.

Libby felt close to tears. She'd been trying not to think about Max, and the danger he might be in. The chance to help Mrs Atkins had seemed like the perfect antidote to her fears. Instead, yet again, she'd been told to keep her nose out of other people's business.

She'd try to cheer herself up that afternoon, with a trip to Alan Jenkins' garage, to have a look at the car.

* * *

Alan worked from a small garage just outside Exham, where he kept his personal collection of classic cars.

As usual, he was lying on his back underneath a Renault Clio, apparently oblivious to the chill in the workshop. Just one small two-bar electric heater struggled to warm the space. A cup of tea steamed on a small table, next to a box of Libby's chocolates.

Alan, it seemed, was developing something of an addiction to them.

He slid out, wiping his hands on an oily rag. 'My favourite customer,' he said.

'I bet you say that to all the ladies,' Libby replied.

'I meant Bear.' He snorted with laughter.

Libby sighed. 'Walked into that, didn't I? Don't you feel the cold?'

He shrugged. 'Thermals. That's the answer.'

Deciding not to delve further into Alan's clothes, Libby asked to see the car he'd reserved for her.

He hesitated. 'Are you sure?'

'Have you sold it?'

'Not exactly.' He shifted from one foot to the other. 'I mean, someone wants it, but it's still – um – available, I suppose. It's a great little car. Come and see. You'll love it.'

She doubted that. She loved her Citroen, with all its faults; its tendency to clam up in cold weather, and its perennially sticky clutch that even Alan had despaired of fixing. All other cars were just a way to get from A to B.

Alan beckoned her into the area he called his showroom, but which Libby would characterise as a shed. 'There she is.'

Libby whistled. A Jeep. An orange Jeep. She'd never even thought of such a vehicle. She felt the smile creep across her face. Now, that would be fun to drive. More fun than Max's Land Rover, with far more character than his Jaguar.

'One careful owner,' Alan announced. 'She brought it in, and I thought of you.'

'Anyone I know?'

'Lady who lives in Bath. Wanted something smaller. A town runabout.' He wrinkled his nose. Alan wasn't a fan of the city.

Libby climbed inside the car. It felt like home. She fiddled with switches that turned on lights and set the wipers going.

'Want to go for a run? I'll look after Bear.'

She set off through narrow lanes under a grey sky, concentrating. Six gears? She was going to enjoy this car.

As she returned, another car drew up on the short stretch of gravel Alan called his forecourt.

'Annabel. Nice to see you.' Libby climbed down from the driver's seat.

Annabel's face was pink. 'Hello? Is that yours?'

'It will be, very soon. I'm going to haggle with Alan.' 'Haggling with Alan,' meant persuading him to charge a reasonable price, rather than giving the car to her at cost. 'But you go first.'

'Oh no. I'm not in a hurry. Just wanted to – er – to book a service. I'll wait outside.'

'In this weather? Nonsense. I'll go round the lanes again for five minutes.'

She returned just in time to wave as Annabel drove away.

'Alan, I adore this car, and I have to own it.'

'Too late.'

'What? You've sold it?'

Alan coughed. 'Well. Promised it.'

'To Annabel?' Libby accused.

'No. Look, Libby, can't explain just now. It needs a bit of work.' That was clearly a lie. What was the matter with the man?

'Well, I can wait until I come back from my honeymoon, I suppose. I won't really need it until then. The Citroen might keep limping along for a while. Can I have first refusal?'

'Course you can.'

Libby left, shaking her head. Alan had always been eccentric, but he seemed to be taking leave of his senses. And he'd finished the chocolates. The box had disappeared. She'd give him an even bigger box for Christmas.

30

NAMING

Libby woke early on Tuesday – the day the Exham on Sea café was due to open.

Robert phoned to explain that the family trees were almost done, and he'd bring them round this evening along with Sarah and a takeaway, because he was sure neither Libby nor Max would want to cook after the first day in the new café.

She loaded up the Citroen, and the little car Mandy drove for the chocolate business, and the two of them processed carefully into town, parking in the small car park behind the new café.

Frank walked down the road to greet them. 'The first day of my retirement,' he said, his face almost split in two by a beaming smile. 'I'll bring the missis in for coffee later, and then we're off for a holiday in Torquay. She wants us to buy a place there, a nice bungalow, for our retirement.'

'You're leaving Exham?' Frank had lived there forever.

'It'll be a wrench, but the missis will be happy.'

Angela, as cool as a cucumber, was already inside the building, smoothing tablecloths and rearranging pictures on the walls.

Gladys arrived with buckets full of plants. 'Difficult to lay my hands on anything fresh, at this time of year,' she told Libby. 'Apart from Christmas trees and holly wreaths, and Angela thinks that's not quite what she needs.' She waved her arm at the palm tree positioned in the corner of the room. 'I brought that over yesterday.'

At the back of the café, the local school's steel band played Caribbean music.

Angela said, 'I thought we'd all had enough of Noddy Holder singing "It's Christmas". I've heard it in every shop in town.'

Libby's hips swayed to the beat. 'All we need is sand, and we'll think we're on a tropical island, not Exham in midwinter. We'll all be dancing by lunchtime.'

Behind the counter lay a long object, wrapped in a sheet.

'The sign,' Angela told Libby. 'We're announcing the winner of the competition to name the café at eleven o'clock, and Owen's sent a man to hang it over the door.'

'Did I win?' Libby asked.

Angela narrowed her eyes. 'What name did you choose?'

'Time for Tea.'

Angela snorted. 'Definitely not.'

'Give me a hint?'

With a shake of the head, Angela drifted away to supervise Annabel, who was in charge of coffee.

Mandy whispered to Libby, 'She wanted to have "Barista" printed on the back of her blouse, but Angela refused. She said, "This is an old-fashioned seaside tea-shop, not a branch of Starbucks."'

Libby, Mandy and Annabel took up their stations behind the counter, and Angela flung open the door, its bell tinkling cheer-fully. 'Welcome, everyone.' She smiled at the small group of

Exham on Sea residents gathered outside, stamping their feet to keep warm. 'Come inside.'

Libby and Mandy retired to the kitchen, their new domain. 'Perfect,' Libby said.

She had to admire Angela's organisation. At one end of the counter, a new, young assistant sold bread, baked to Frank's recipes, along with freshly cut sandwiches. Annabel waited at the tables, with Angela's assistance planned for busier moments, supplying toasted teacakes and slices of chocolate cake, while Mandy lurked behind a glass case containing Mrs Forest's Chocolates, weighing them out to folk who'd 'just popped in' but had 'no time to stop for coffee'.

Even Dr Sheffield arrived, to buy a dozen doughnuts, 'For the surgery.' He'd never before darkened the bakery's doors, and Libby watched, fascinated, as Annabel served him, blushing and twinkling. No wonder there was no love lost between her and Joanna.

Libby grabbed Angela's arm as her friend paused to catch her breath. 'This is going to be a success.'

'You may be right.' Angela glowed. She crossed her fingers. 'We won't know until later in the year – it's full today, because it's the opening. We need to find out if the summer holiday visitors like it.'

A clock chimed.

'Eleven o'clock. Time for the official naming ceremony.' Angela tapped a spoon against a cup, to gain everyone's attention.

The chocolate cake was down to its last slice, and needed to be replaced. Libby slipped back into the kitchen to prepare a second plateful.

She slid the replacement carefully from its box, transferred it to a cake stand, and turned to pick up a sharp knife, ready to slice it into neat portions.

She raised the knife.

A hand closed over her mouth.

'Don't move.' No more than a grunt.

A second fist gripped her fingers, forcing the knife from her grasp. It clattered on the floor.

Libby tried to turn her head, but the hand squeezed her face, crushing her lips painfully against her teeth.

She fumbled for the phone in her pocket, tried to pull it out, but it slipped from her hand and crashed to the floor.

'Keep quiet.' That was a different voice.

Libby stood rigid. Had the second man picked up the knife? It would slice through her neck, as through butter.

A hood, dark and smelling of damp burlap, slid over her head, blocking out the light. The two men lifted her easily, as if she were no heavier than a tray of new-baked bread.

She fought to stay calm, not daring to cry out, as they carried her through the kitchen door and dropped her into the boot of a car waiting directly outside the kitchen. The boot slammed shut.

Trying to breathe steadily, to calm the panic that rose inside and made her heart thump, she thought. *If they kill me, I'll never know what the café's going to be called.*

She muttered, aloud. 'They're not going to kill you. Don't be ridiculous,' but still she had to clench her fists to stop herself screaming. No one would hear her inside the car boot.

'Think,' she urged. 'Who are they?'

Had she recognised the voices? The men had hardly spoken – just a few words. Had she heard a Somerset burr, or was she imagining things?

With a jerk, the car set off, throwing her around the boot, her elbow cracking painfully against the side of her prison.

What kind of car was this? It was bigger than her Citroen –

you couldn't have fitted a child in that boot – but not as big as Max's Land Rover.

It rocked around bends, tossing her from side to side, slowed to take a longer bend, and sped up. The motorway. She calculated she was on the M5, headed either south, to Taunton and Devon, or north, towards Bristol.

31

FAMILY TREES

On the morning of the café opening, Max lay awake. Last night, after hours on the internet, he'd discovered a scrap of information that he could hardly wait to take to Libby. He'd been trying to find something – anything – about Ivor Wrighton, but it seemed the man had hardly existed online. That was suspicious in itself – everyone had some kind of online presence.

Then, he'd had an idea. Stella had given Ivor those handkerchiefs as one of his birthday presents. Knowing Stella, there would be a photo somewhere in her own footprint. She took photographs of everything to post on Facebook.

He'd turned to her Facebook page and scrutinised every photograph, tracing them to her posts.

At last, 'Bingo,' he'd shouted. There was Stella, in a selfie with Ivor, holding up one of the handkerchiefs. But, it was the date that fascinated Max. 10 July.

Ivor's birthday was on 10 July, The date rang a bell.

Max pulled up his earlier research into Carys' missing son, Maurice. 'Praise be!' he exclaimed. Maurice and Ivor shared a birthday.

It wasn't conclusive, but it was an exciting coincidence.

Was Ivor Wrighton actually Maurice Noakes? He was Welsh, with the same birthday as Carys' son. And he'd been murdered, like Carys.

Max would be willing to bet the house he was the same man.

Libby was going to be so excited.

It didn't tell Max who the murderer – the Rhymer – was, though.

Those poison-pen letters from the sixties niggled at his mind. Did they hold a vital clue? Had they given the present-day Rhymer his idea?

Max couldn't wait until the evening before seeing the results of Robert's research. He was on a roll, and he'd try to finish the job.

Libby was busy, today, at the café opening, but he could visit her son and see what his genealogical dive into the past had uncovered. He'd call Robert and see if he was free.

Sure enough, Robert, who worked from home, was delighted to take an hour to indulge in his favourite hobby.

'Sorry, dogs, I shall do this alone,' Max announced. 'I'll take you out this afternoon.'

Robert greeted Max with enthusiasm and several sheets of paper, the size of billowing sails, that covered the floor.

They wasted no time on chit-chat, Robert jumping right in. 'I don't know if any of this helps, but it's fascinating. Let me show you.' He rubbed his hands together. 'I've drawn up a tree for each of the people who received a poison-pen letter in the sixties. Here's an example – Henry Trelawney. Henry lived all his life in Exham, married a woman called Elizabeth James and had two sons – Malcolm and Gavin, in 1959 and 1961. They have a couple of children each, born in different parts of the country.'

Max nodded. 'I was at school with Gavin Trelawney. He was a few years older than me, though, so I don't remember much about him.' Nevertheless, he made a note of the names on his phone.

'Right,' Robert said. 'That's an easy tree, because the names all fit. Names can be a trap. Until recently, English children nearly always took their father's surname, if the father was on the scene. If not, they usually share a name with the mother. If there's a divorce and remarriage – or even two...'

'I see what you mean. It can get complicated.'

Robert was enjoying himself. 'It can. If a woman marries twice, her children often have different last names, and that's turned out to be the case with several of these Exham families.'

Max glanced through the neatly drawn diagrams. 'This is going to take a while. I want to cross-check the names from the sixties with the people in my ex-wife's list of friends. Can I take these with me?' He gestured towards the papers blanketing the floor. 'I've got to go if I'm to arrive at the café in time for the grand naming ceremony, and I daren't be late. Your mother will eat me alive.'

'I can do better than that,' Robert said. 'I'll scan them and email them to you.'

* * *

Max made it to the café just in time. Annabel handed him a tiny glass of celebratory Prosecco, the steel band sounded a fanfare, and Owen handed Angela a microphone.

Libby was nowhere to be seen.

Angela announced, 'The winning name in the competition to name our new café is... The Crusts and Crumbs Café.' Amid applause, she went on, 'And the person who suggested it is

Joanna Sheffield. So, let's raise our glasses to the success of Exham's new café, The Crusts and Crumbs Café.'

Where was Libby hiding?

Max crossed the room to Mandy. 'Where's Libby? She won't want to miss this.'

'I saw her go into the kitchen a few minutes ago. I'll get her.' She put her head round the door into the kitchen, but returned, shrugging her shoulders. 'Nope, not there. Maybe in the ladies'?'

Hairs rose on the back of Max's neck. This felt wrong. 'Could you look?'

Mandy walked to the side and opened the door to the washrooms, emerging a few moments later. 'No one there at the moment. Maybe she went out the back for a breath of fresh air. It's been hectic in here.' She dived back through the door into the kitchen, and, seconds later, ran back out, eyes wide in a white face. 'The back door's open and... and there's a knife lying on the floor in the kitchen, beside Libby's phone.'

Max pushed past Annabel.

'Staff only,' she cried, but he scowled and her voice died away.

The kitchen was deserted.

He snatched Libby's phone and tried to turn it on, but the battery was dead.

He hurried through the kitchen and out of the door at the back. The small car park was full. There was Libby's car, beside Mandy's runabout, and he recognised Angela's car at the end of the row.

But what caught his attention was a skid mark, close to the door. A car had left recently – travelling fast.

'Mandy, was there a car here this morning?'

'Not that I remember, but I've been inside for hours. Maybe one of the others knows. I'll ask.'

'Be discreet. We don't want to cause alarm on Angela's big day.

Not unless we have to.'

Mandy slipped quietly round the room, talking to staff under cover of the babble of noise. They shook their heads. 'No one's seen anything,' she told Max.

'Let's try the other shops in the road.' Max was icy calm, determined not to panic. Why shouldn't Libby have popped out onto the high street? She was always leaving her phone around and often forgot to charge it up. Besides, there was nothing unusual about a dropped knife in a café kitchen. But the knife and the phone, together on the floor, told a different story.

Max left by the front door, Mandy close behind. She turned right and Max, left, working his way along the street, eyes sweeping the interior of each shop. The town was almost deserted. Most of Exham was in the café, toasting its first day.

'Have you seen Libby Forest?' Max asked the young lad at the hardware shop.

He shook his head and sniggered. 'Lost her already, have you – and not even married, yet.'

Max had no patience for jokes. 'Tell her we're looking for her,' he ordered, and tried the estate agents.

Freddy sat at the desk nearest the door, lounging back, his arms behind his neck.

'Hope you're a customer,' he grinned. 'It's never been so quiet.' No Libby.

'Have you seen any cars speeding away from the town, this morning?'

Freddy guffawed. 'Like in *Top Gear*? I don't think so. Nothing like that goes on here. My dad was right – I should have got a job in Bristol, at that new games arcade. That's where things happen.'

Max returned to the café. He could no longer pretend all was well.

Libby had gone.

32

HUMPTY DUMPTY

Max met Mandy back at the café.

She shook her head. 'Nothing. She's just disappeared. Are you going to call the police?'

He hesitated. 'She's only been gone a short while, and she's a grown woman.'

'Yes, but you two work for the police, don't you? Doesn't that make a difference?'

'Maybe it does, at that.'

He called DCI Morrison's phone.

The officer listened calmly. 'So, you're thinking her disappearance is connected to these emails I've been hearing so much about, from my DC Humberstone, and the murders we're working on.'

'Maybe.' A shiver ran through Max.

'Right. Your fiancée does have a way of getting herself into dangerous spots, doesn't she? I'll get one of my people from the Carys Evans enquiry to look into it, since Libby's one of our own. You go home. We can't have you buzzing around the country like a bluebottle. If you have any bright ideas, let me know.'

It was good advice, but Max couldn't bear to do nothing. His instinct was to get in the car and drive around, desperately searching for a strange vehicle, but he knew that was a foolish gut reaction. Whoever had taken Libby could be miles away by now.

Fighting the urge to run, he returned to the café. 'I expect she's thought of something and run off to deal with it,' he said, trying to sound calm. 'You know what she's like.'

'I suppose so.' Mandy sounded sceptical, but customers were waiting. 'Let me know when you find her,' she hissed, and went back to work.

Max sat in his car, wondering what to do. He checked his phone, even though he knew Libby's phone was dead, so there could be no message from her. He scrolled down his emails and froze.

A new message.

From 'a well-wisher'.

Max read it through and a stone settled in his stomach.

Want her safe? Come and get her. You like mysteries – all you have to do is follow the clues. Like on your computer – nice photos of the ex-wife, by the way.

Clues? Where had they taken her?

Max swallowed hard. He'd been right, that day when Fuzzy had escaped. The Rhymer had been in his house, and he'd hacked into his password-protected PC. Whoever was doing this knew a thing or two about computers.

He closed his eyes. The Rhymer could have killed him then, or the animals, but he hadn't? Why? He could only suppose it was because the Rhymer had other plans, and those plans involved Libby.

But what of Stella? The email mentioned her as well. What was the Rhymer up to?

He scrolled down the screen on his phone. Another email pinged in. The subject was: *Another clue.*

Max read the new rhyme.

> Humpty Dumpty sat on a wall
> Humpty Dumpty had a great fall
> All the king's horses and all the king's men
> Couldn't put Humpty together again.

A fall? Was Libby going to fall somewhere? But, where, and why? Somewhere high, like a tower or a railway bridge? Max shivered, seeing her in his imagination lying on train tracks at Highbridge station as a Great Western Railway train thundered towards her.

He took a deep breath. Panic would help nobody.

There was no sense in replying to the message. He'd just have to wait.

As if reading his mind, his email pinged again.

Think you got away with it, don't you?

What did that mean?

He sat back, tapping his fingers on the wheel. He was being accused of something, but he had no idea what it could be.

He looked again at the email, and swore.

It was addressed to him, but everyone in Exham who'd received a nursery rhyme had been copied in. They'd all see the accusation against Max.

But, accused of what? Sending the rhymes?

That was crazy, but it made him feel sick.

He waited, but no more emails arrived. What about social media?

With a sinking sensation, he turned to Facebook. Sure enough, he found a sequence of posts attacking him.

Anyone know why Max Ramshore's trolling us?
If you've had an insulting rhyme, blame Max Ramshore.
Here's a guy who thinks it's funny to bad-mouth local people…

He tried other sites – Twitter, Instagram. Everywhere, the story was the same. Dozens of posts, all accusing Max of stalking and trolling the neighbours.

The anonymous email-sender had branched out in a big way, and he – or she – was out to ruin Max's reputation.

He could block the accounts, but he knew that as fast as he did that, more would pop up. Whoever was doing this knew how to set up false accounts too fast to be stopped. Fake news, that's what it was called and it could be devastating. People's lives had been ruined by a few malicious social media posts.

Anger boiled up in Max, but he forced himself to keep calm. The slurs were nasty and spiteful, but he was far more worried about Libby.

More Tweets appeared:

How did Carys Evans die? Shouldn't the police ask Max?
Ivor Wrighton died because of one man – a certain Max Ramshore.

This was deeply personal. The writer of rhymes, the Nursery Rhymer, had taken off the gloves at last and stopped playing games. He meant business, now, and it seemed Max was the focus of his venom.

Did the Rhymer have Libby? What would he do with her?

He breathed deliberately, fighting fear. Two people were already dead. What if the Rhymer's next act would be to hurt Libby and lay the blame on Max?

He needed to think – think logically.

Whoever was sending the rhymes knew the victims. Most lived in Exham – but not all. Stella, his ex-wife, had received one, along with other strange emails.

Stella. Why target her?

Max's head was spinning. He was wasting time. Libby was in danger, but he had no idea where she could be.

He grasped at straws. The police would track her down. They'd identify the car that had driven away from Exham at the time she disappeared, and trace its progress. It could be done, he knew, but it would take time.

And time was a luxury he didn't have.

He needed to check on Stella. He rang Stella's number, but the call went to voicemail.

He tried Joe.

'Hey, Dad. What's this about Libby? Mandy rang to say she's missing.'

Max explained, as calmly as he could, and cut through Joe's exclamations. 'Joe, is your mum with you?'

'No, she left yesterday. Said she felt better and wanted to get home. She seemed to recover from her friend's death pretty quickly, I have to say. Maybe it wasn't the big romance, after all. Oh, she had a call to say she'd left a scarf or something in the Bristol hotel, and she planned to call in on the way and pick it up. You know what she's like about clothes. But can I help with finding Libby? Any idea where she might be?'

Max's hand shook as he listened. It may be nonsense, but... 'Wait a bit, I need to make another call.'

Seconds later, he was talking to the receptionist at the Avon Gorge Hotel.

'No, sorry. We've no record of any lost property for that room; there would be a note on the computer. Let me just check with my colleague.' Max heard muffled voices and the receptionist returned. 'Definitely no lost property. I'm so sorry.'

Max thought for a second. Had Stella been into the hotel since she left? Yesterday, perhaps? He asked the receptionist.

'There's nothing in the records. I hope she's well?' The girl was beginning to sound worried.

'She's fine, I'm sure.' He had an idea. 'Do you have CCTV on your car park?'

'We do. It's run by our security people. Shall I put you through?'

'Please.'

A few minutes later, a deep voice and broad Bristol accent came on the line. 'Can I help you, sir?'

Max explained. 'My ex-wife had a bereavement a few days ago and she's not answering her phone. I'm a little worried. She was very upset. I'm trying to track her down and I think she may have been in your car park yesterday afternoon.' Max calculated the time Stella had left Joe and her journey time. 'Sometime after two o'clock. Could you check the CCTV footage?'

He gave the car make and registration.

'I'll have a look and let you know.'

Max waited, telling himself it would take ages for the guard to run through the tapes, but his phone rang within minutes.

'I had a look in the car park, and the car's there, sir, but our receptionist tells me the owner is no longer booked into the hotel.'

'I'm on my way. I'll be with you as soon as I can. And keep looking through the CCTV.'

'Yes, sir.'

Ignoring speed limits, Max roared along the motorway, his brain working at a furious rate.

Libby and Stella both missing. Carys and Ivor both dead. Max himself under attack, being blamed for the nursery rhyme emails.

A theory began to form. He looked at it from all sides. It seemed crazy – but that didn't make it untrue. All the facts fitted and all the links fell into place, one by one, like a jigsaw.

His tyres squealed as he turned into the hotel car park. Sure enough, there was Stella's car.

The security guard greeted him, excited, his words falling over each other. 'Come and look, sir. It's on camera.'

The black and white footage was clear enough. Riveted, Max watched as Stella's car pulled into the car park. As soon as she'd parked, a battered 4x4 drew up close to the driver's door. Stella pushed her door open, frowning, annoyed. A man appeared from the driver's side of the 4x4, his head obscured by a cloth cap.

The irritation on Stella's face switched to fear as the man grabbed her arm. She tried to pull away. He said something and she stopped struggling. Her head twisted from side to side as though searching for help, but the man dragged her round the car and shoved her into the back seat.

The angle was difficult, but Max was sure he could see another figure, face hidden, beside her in the car.

Max whistled. He looked at the footage again, and then once more. There was something familiar about the man who'd taken Stella's arm. The way he moved? His height?

Max didn't recognise the 4x4, and the number plate was obscured by muddy splashes.

He sat back, putting two and two together, making far more than four, and wondering what on earth to do next.

33

SANDWICH

Libby's journey seemed to last for hours, but she knew it was probably far less than that. Her head ached from crashing repeatedly against the side of the boot, and the sack made breathing difficult. She tried to remove it, but the kidnapper had tied it round her neck and she had little room to manoeuvre. Giving up the attempt, she took long, slow breaths, and tried to stay calm.

She felt the car leave the motorway and travel along smaller roads until, at last, it drew to a halt.

She wished they were still driving. At least, in the boot of the car she was safe from her captors.

Shoes crunched on gravel and the boot flew open.

'Out you get,' growled one of her captors. Libby struggled out of the boot.

The man grabbed her arm and dragged her up a short path. She heard keys in a lock. Still gripping her arm, he pushed her, blind, through a door, along a stretch of uncarpeted floor, and turned her to the left.

'Upstairs,' he grunted. Libby was sure she'd heard that voice before.

She stumbled on the stairs and only the grip on her arm stopped her falling.

Once at the top, her captor fumbled with her hood, pulled it off and shoved her forward, slamming the door behind her. From outside, he called, 'Keep quiet and you'll be all right.'

Her eyes felt gritty and itchy, from the sacking. She sneezed, and looked round. She was in a small room, an ordinary bedroom, in what appeared to be a suburban house. A bed with a bare mattress stood against the wall on one side of the room. The room was painted a cheerful yellow, as though it had at one time been a child's bedroom, but the paint was scratched and peeling. A couple of torn alphabet stickers remained, still clinging forlornly to the wall under a window. A single, wooden chair stood by a table bearing a jug of water, a tin cup, and a plate covered by a cloth. She pulled off the cloth. Sandwiches.

She fought a hysterical desire to laugh at the anticlimax. She'd been kidnapped, driven in a state of terror for miles, and then left in a room with a ham sandwich. No handcuffs? No ties on her ankles?

These men were amateurs.

But why had she been brought here? What did they want from her?

She ran back to the door and hammered on it, shouting, 'Let me out this minute.'

The almost-familiar voice on the other side snapped, 'Keep your voice down. I don't want to have to shut you up.'

He sounded as though he meant it.

Libby stopped shouting.

She stood back, and looked round again. At the foot of the bed was a second door. She strode across and grabbed the handle. The door swung open and she found herself in a small en suite bathroom with another door that, she supposed, led out of the bathroom into the upstairs passageway. Hopefully, she rattled the handle, but the door was locked.

At least she wouldn't have to suffer the indignity of wetting herself.

Footsteps tramped down the stairs, but so far as she could tell, no door opened. Her captors were still in the house.

How could she escape? The bedroom's large sash window looked big enough for her to climb through. She peered out, hopeful, but a straight drop fell to a paved path under the window. She'd break her legs if she jumped.

She thought of old films she'd seen. Captives often made their escape by tying sheets together. Unfortunately, there were no sheets on the bed and no curtains at the window. Maybe these amateur kidnappers were more efficient than she'd supposed. She disliked that idea.

The small bathroom boasted a tiny, frosted window that even Shipley would find impossible to navigate. She'd have to find her way out via the bedroom door.

Libby rattled the handle, gently, to avoid making a noise, but the door was locked from the other side. She bent down and peered through the keyhole. To her delight, the key was still in the lock. She'd surely have no trouble dislodging that so that it fell on the floor. It would fall on the wrong side of the door, but along with any keen reader of Nancy Drew Mysteries, The Famous Five, or Agatha Christie, she knew how to deal with that.

She needed a sheet of paper. Her handbag, always full of scrunched-up bills and leaflets, as well as her trusty notebook, remained under the counter of the café in Exham on Sea.

She wasted a moment wondering whether anyone had noticed her absence. Was Max even now on her track? But he'd have no idea where to come.

She wrenched her thoughts away from Max. It didn't help to dwell on him. He'd be worried sick.

'Think about solving the problem,' she muttered.

She beamed. The ham sandwich was in a bag.

'Didn't think of that, did you?' she whispered, tipping the food out on to the plate.

Her spirits rose. She smoothed the paper and slid it under the door, finding that wasn't as easy as she'd expected. It kept sticking on the carpet. Finally, she managed to manoeuvre it into place, and turned her attention to the lock.

She had no implement thin enough to slide through the keyhole to push the key from the lock. If only she had Max's lock-picking kit. He'd bought it once, as a joke, and it had come in useful. If she ever got out of here, she'd buy one of her own.

Just then, Libby heard voices. A door opened below and a foot trod on the stairs. They were coming.

She whisked the paper bag back from under the door and just had time to drop it on the table before the door opened.

One of her captors, wearing a woollen face mask with holes for his eyes, stood in the doorway, arms folded.

'What do you want?' she asked, hoping to sound confident, but the wobble in her voice betrayed her.

The man laughed. 'Never you mind.'

To hide her legs, which were shaking, Libby sat down on the chair.

'Is it money?' That was better. She'd kept the tremble from her voice.

He laughed. 'Just settle down and wait. Now, don't you want your sandwich? Not special enough for the famous Mrs Forest?' There was a hard edge of malice in his voice.

'Not hungry,' she said.

'Suit yourself.' He approached the table. 'You'll be sorry later.'

Libby calculated. Could she get between him and the door and run? But his mate was still downstairs. She couldn't deal with two of them at once.

She stayed where she was.

He took the sandwich and the paper bag and left.

Libby was shaking. She'd managed to hide her terror, but it had been an act.

'Think sensibly,' she scolded herself. If they'd left food, they weren't about to kill her. Not yet, anyway.

She couldn't just sit about and wait, but he'd taken the paper bag and spoiled her plan. She'd have to start again.

In the bathroom, there was a roll of toilet paper, but it was flimsy stuff. She tore off several sheets and tried to slide them under the bedroom door, but they wouldn't hold their shape against the friction from the carpet.

What about the bathroom door? That, too, had a key on the other side of the lock, but there was no carpet in the bathroom to stop the paper sliding.

It glided easily over the tiled floor and disappeared under the door.

Now she needed that implement, long and thin enough to fit into the keyhole. Wire. She needed a strand of wire.

She searched every inch of the bathroom before trying the plastic shower curtain. It was supported by wire hoops. She could have cheered.

It was easy enough to straighten out one of the hoops and insert it into the keyhole, but the minutes ticked away as she tried to wiggle the key out of the lock. It was far more difficult than it seemed in films.

Her fingers ached, but there was no time to rest.

At last, the wire slid into position. She twisted it, and felt the key turn in the lock. A final flick and push dislodged the key and it fell onto the paper.

Holding her breath, praying the gap under the door was wide enough for the key to fit underneath, she slid the paper towards her. Gently, carefully, she edged it closer, until the key appeared.

Triumphantly, she scrabbled it into her hand, unlocked the door, pushed it open a fraction, held her breath, and listened.

34

THE CHOICE

Sitting in his car, Max refreshed his emails, over and over again. 'Come on,' he muttered.

The waiting, for another clue from the kidnappers, was unbearable. He needed to act. Do something.

But, what could he do?

Think, he told himself. *Work it through.*

Libby and Stella had both been taken. Where were they being kept? Were they together? Were they hurt?

He told himself they'd be fine. Their captor must have a plan. They'd be no use to him dead.

He tried hard not to listen to the voice in the back of his head that told him this was all his fault. But he didn't know who wanted to ruin his reputation, or why they'd taken the two most important women in his life.

His email pinged.

Time to choose, Max. Which are you going to save – the old wife, or the new?

He tasted bile at the back of his mouth.

Follow the clues. Then, say goodbye to one or the other.

His email buzzed again and two photos appeared – one of Libby and the other, Stella. Each sat, wide-eyed, on a wooden chair. Max looked closely. They looked dishevelled, and scared, but at least neither appeared seriously hurt.

Here they are, in case you think we're bluffing. Which one's for the high jump? You choose.

High jump? That was one of the clues, but what did it mean? *Don't rush off*, he told himself. *Ignore the death threat. Think it through.*

Head in hands, he sat for ten minutes, considering everything he knew.

Two deaths. He was being set up as the Rhymer and the killer, but he needed to get past that thought. Carys Evans died first. Why? What pushed a man or woman to kill? Jealousy, rage, money, protecting someone, or some psychological flaw? He'd come across all those motives. The motive he found hardest to understand was that of a killer who murders 'because he can'. Someone who's lost contact with the real world and sees a murder as an exciting challenge to be overcome. Which of these applied to the Rhymer?

Money? Ivor had plenty, and Carys had surprised everyone by leaving a substantial amount in her will. Did that lead anywhere?

There was something like an itch in Max's brain as he thought that through. A sentence that had surprised him when he heard it. But what was he struggling to remember? Who'd talked about money? What had they said? Had they been talking to Max, or was it something Libby had mentioned?

He beat his fists against his head in frustration. 'Think,' he muttered.

He closed his eyes and tracked back to the day he'd found Carys in the woods. He thought through every conversation he could remember from the past two weeks, no matter how trivial it had seemed at the time.

That was when he remembered.

Shocked, he tried to think of another solution, but there was one person who fitted all the circumstances.

He remembered Robert's family trees. He hadn't thought about those since discovering Libby had been snatched, but if his suspicions were correct, they'd tell him what he needed to know.

Max opened up the attachment Robert had sent, scrolled down all the names, and stopped.

'Robert,' he murmured. 'You're a genius.' It was, as Robert had suggested, all about the names. Names that could be changed.

In Max's brain, cogs turned and connections fell into place.

Ivor Wrighton, as Max was sure, was also Maurice Noakes; Carys Evans' son with her first husband, Peter Noakes. After leaving prison and making a new life, Maurice had changed his name. He might have wanted to go straight, and leave his old life behind, but he'd found it easier to live at other people's expense. He'd probably moved from one wealthy older woman to another, living off their money, changing his name each time to keep ahead of the law, ending with Stella.

But Maurice/Ivor had died. He couldn't be the Rhymer.

Who, then, had killed both Maurice/Ivor and his mother?

Max sat back, his eyes closed, trying to make sense of the puzzle.

Names, marriages, family trees – he opened his eyes. He hadn't finished looking at Louise Barnet's tree. He'd stopped when he came to Maurice's name.

Louise Barnet, one of the recipients of the poison pen letters, had a family tree that divided into two branches, because she had married twice.

With her first husband, she'd had one daughter. Newly divorced, she'd then moved to Wales with a second husband, John Evans, where two more daughters had been born – Gladys and Carys. They'd each reverted to their maiden name of Evans when their own marriages broke down.

It was Louise's first marriage that Max wanted to explore. He scrolled down the page, and gasped. Louise's eldest daughter had married a man called Redditch, and they'd had a son.

That son's name jumped out at Max as though it was written in red capital letters: Oliver Redditch, his own old school friend. He thought back to their conversation on the seafront at Watchet. Ollie had admitted he'd had a hard time, lately. He was down on his luck. He'd lost his job; his 'nice little earner', his 'under-the-radar' work, hacking commercial companies for the shady firm, Pritchards... which had been shut down, because of Max and Libby's investigations. Was that his motive? Fury that they'd ruined his life? Was he out for revenge?

But Ollie was Max's old mate from school. They'd shared cheese sandwiches in the playground, played football together, spent Saturday evenings at the Odeon in Bristol, trying to pick up girls. Why would Max's old friend have turned against him like this? Kidnapping Libby? Taunting and killing people? Spreading vile rumours about Max?

And, why kill Carys Evans, his aunt?

Rocked to his core, Max replayed the Watchet conversation

with Ollie in his head, and re-read the emails about Libby's kidnap.

That day in Watchet, Ollie had said his aunt gave him money.

Ollie had been broke – ruined by the collapse of Pritchards, the company Libby and Max had exposed. His wife had left. His life had fallen apart.

His aunt's money had helped him back on his feet. Max only had Ollie's word for it that his aunt had lent him money. What if he'd stolen it from her? He'd have access to her house – after all, she was family. What if he'd stayed with her? Nothing could be easier than stealing a credit card from her house. She probably kept a book beside the computer with passwords in it – so many people did. Once he'd found that, a scammer like Ollie would be able to move money from her account into his.

Max took it a step further. What if Aunt Carys found the money missing, put two and two together, and threatened Ollie with the police if he didn't pay her back?

So, Ollie had killed her. Not as bad as killing your mother, but shocking enough.

But she wouldn't have left her money to him, because she had a son of her own. Maurice. Maurice Noakes, the bad boy, the black sheep, also known as Ivor Wrighton

Had Maurice/Ivor found out that Ollie, his cousin, had killed Carys, his mother?

Max shrugged into his coat, sure now that Ollie was behind the rhymes – Ollie, the computer expert, who loved playing games, who'd lost his money and his wife, who'd stolen more and couldn't afford to pay it back. Ollie, who'd killed his aunt because she'd threatened him with the law. Ollie, who hated Max and Libby for their part in his bankruptcy.

Max knew, now, where Ollie would take the two women. The emails had mentioned a fall. Carys and Ivor had both been found in Leigh Woods. The Avon Gorge. There was only one place to look.

One mystery remained: Why had Ollie killed his cousin, Maurice/Ivor?

Max left a note for the helpful security guard, with instructions to ring the police, jumped in his car, and sped away.

35

SURPRISE

Libby, outside the bathroom, could hear the murmur of voices downstairs, but she had no idea of the layout of the house, or whether the two men could see the stairs.

There was another closed door on the other side of the short landing. Maybe that one would have a window from which she could jump without breaking her ankles.

More noise from downstairs. Water running and cupboard doors opening and shutting. The men must be in the kitchen.

She listened again. Their voices echoed a little, so that she could make out what they were saying.

'Did he pick up the latest message?'

'He did.' The second man sniggered. 'Bet he's chasing around, trying to work out where she is.'

'You're right. Are they safe up there?'

'Safe as houses.' He sniggered again.

They? Had Libby heard correctly?

She tiptoed across to the other door. It was locked, but once again the key was on the outside.

Libby turned the key and gently twisted the handle. The door swung open, revealing a room almost the twin of hers.

A woman sat on the single chair. As Libby entered, the woman's head jerked up.

Libby caught her breath. Another gang member?

But, the woman's clothes, expensive-looking, were creased and crumpled. Her hair was dishevelled, half in and half out of a chignon, strands hanging over her face. She'd been crying.

Another prisoner.

Libby whispered, 'What's going on?' She crossed the room, half an ear on the voices downstairs. Listening in case one of the men came upstairs.

The other woman flinched.

'I'm not one of them,' Libby said. 'Who are you?'

The other woman blew her nose and said, 'My name's Stella and I've been kidnapped.'

'Stella?' Libby squinted at her. 'Stella? Not Max's ex-wife?'

Stella sniffed. 'And you are?' There was a trace of haughtiness in her voice.

'Libby Forest.'

Stella's eyes narrowed. She looked Libby up and down. 'What are you doing here?' She raised an eyebrow, and Libby found herself brushing imaginary dust from her own jumper.

'I suspect, the same thing as you. I've been kidnapped.' She paused. 'How long have you been here?'

'Overnight,' Stella said 'And all they've given me is one very unpleasant sandwich.'

Despite their predicament, the outrage in her voice made Libby chuckle. 'I think that's the least of our problems. Have you any idea what's going on?'

Fascinated to have met Max's ex at last, despite the weird circumstances, Libby forgot to listen for their captors.

The door suddenly flew open.

'You two ladies have met, then. Very clever, Mrs Forest. You would have enjoyed a spell in the Escape Room at my club. Pity it's too late for that. At least, you two have plenty to talk about. I'll leave you to it. You won't have long to wait. We're all going on a little trip. And some of us will be coming back. Not all, I'm afraid.'

The masked man left, slamming the door, and the key turned in the lock. Libby slumped down, sitting on the floor against the wall. All that effort, and she was back where she'd started – a prisoner.

It was dark when Max arrived at the Clifton Suspension Bridge. He slid the car into a space near the Information Centre and slammed on the brakes.

The area was quiet, now the afternoon rush hour was over. Lights twinkled from houses and flats in the Cumberland Basin, but the bridge itself was dark. Wasn't it meant to be floodlit at night?

The Information Centre was closed. Max's heart sank. Had he misunderstood Ollie's clues? But no, the 4x4 he'd seen in the CCTV coverage was here. Where, then, were Libby and Stella?

Below the bridge, so far down that Max's senses swam at the sight, the edge of the gorge was invisible in the dark. He shivered, but it wasn't the wind that bothered him, although it blew gusts of rain like needles into his face.

He hated heights.

At least the barriers along the walkway, two metres high, gave some sense of safety.

Max knew that, despite the barriers, suicides still took place on the bridge. CCTV had been installed, giving the bridge keepers time to stop many attempts, but tonight, someone had interfered with the bridge's normal working. Someone with the grasp of computer knowledge and hacking ability to get into the systems. Now, he knew he was right. Ollie was here. Ollie, the computer hacker.

A couple of cars drove past and a gust of wind hit Max in the face. He brushed freezing rain from his cheeks.

Then, he saw them. Four figures, merging into the shadow of the wall near the toll booth.

Max shouted, and Ollie turned.

'At last. I thought you'd never get here, Max. Thought maybe you were leaving your women to die of cold.'

'What's the matter with you, Ollie?' Max called into the wind. 'I thought we were mates.'

'You're no friend of mine, Max Ramshore. You and your – your woman,' he spat the words with venom. 'You lost me my job and every penny I owned.'

The other man growled, 'And my marriage.'

Ollie's accomplice, heavily built, had a firm grip on Libby's arm. With a jolt, Max recognised him. Mandy's abusive father.

'Bert?'

In answer, Bert shoved Libby hard against the wall. It reached just above her waist.

Max shook his head. Why was Bert mixed up in this? 'What have we ever done to you?'

Bert jerked his head towards Libby. 'You and her – you think you're so clever, interfering in Exham's business. Well, you broke up my marriage, talking my Elaine into leaving me.'

Libby struggled uselessly against Bert's grip. 'You were beating her up.'

Bert just grunted and crushed Libby harder against the wall.

Max said, 'What do you want, Ollie? What's this all about? Those nursery rhymes – some sort of family tradition, are they?'

Ollie let a slow smile creep over his face. 'You know about my Granny Louise, do you? Took you long enough to work it out. Quite a girl, she was; life and soul of the party. All the men liked her. But when she left her husband and daughter no one in town would talk to her. Stuck-up bunch of nosy parkers in those days – and they haven't changed much, neither. She moved to Wales, married her new man, had Carys and Gladys and broke off all her ties with Exham; apart from sending a few letters to punish those Exham gossips. No one could stop Granny having fun.'

'So, your grandmother, Louise Barnet, sent the poison-pen letters in the sixties?'

Ollie chuckled. 'Only to people who deserved them.'

Every word he spoke confirmed Max's deductions. 'You copied her idea, upgraded it to nursery rhymes and sent one to yourself, just like she'd done, to put people off the scent. I should have realised – you were always mad for games.'

Ollie's laughter drifted away on the wind. 'Those nursery rhymes were all my own work. Best fun I'd had in years. Like a fox in a hen coop, I was, setting all those Exham folk into a proper flutter.' Ollie's laughter changed to a sneer. 'Forest and Ramshore, Private Investigators, couldn't make head nor tail of them.' He pointed his finger in Libby's face. 'You should learn to keep your nose out of other people's business, Libby Forest.'

Max said, 'Didn't your aunts, Carys and Gladys, know about Granny Louise's poison-pen letters? She was their mother, after all.'

'Granny hushed it up. My own mum told me, but she said it was a family secret. Not to tell anyone.'

Amazing. Ollie had been at school with Max, but he'd never once mentioned those letters. He let Ollie talk. If the man got it all off his chest, spilled out the anger and resentment against Exham, and especially Max and Libby, maybe he'd calm down and let the two women go. Although, at the moment, he showed no sign of letting his grip on Stella loosen for a second.

When Ollie spoke again, his voice had lost its bitter edge, but it was harder, more determined. 'Now,' he said, 'it's payback time for you. Come on, Mr Perfect Ramshore, time to choose one of your women. Imagine you're in the Big Brother house. Who do you want to save? The other one's going over the edge.'

Max's heart seemed to stall. Ollie was serious. He'd already murdered two people, and he was planning to kill either Libby or Stella.

Max peered into the blackness. Where were the police? They must be arriving soon. If only the bridge lights would go on. Occasional cars passed over the bridge, oblivious to the drama being played out by the tower, the drivers squinting through the rain, concentrating on their journeys, barely noticing the small group by the wall.

Could Max get help from a passing motorist? He discarded the idea. If he made any false move, Ollie could throw Stella over the low wall in seconds, to certain death in the gorge, far below.

Where were the bridge keepers? Max supposed they were busy trying to sort out the floodlights, unable to see what was happening in the dark.

It was up to him. He must keep Ollie talking until help arrived.

'What I don't understand, Ollie, is why you killed Carys Evans. She was your aunt – or step-aunt – and she'd helped you out with money. Or did you help yourself? A spot of identity theft?'

'Useful things, credit cards,' Ollie sniggered. 'I used one to get into your posh house, as well. Slid it into the lock on your French doors. Easy as pie. That was fun, snooping around. Good protection on your PC, though. Didn't find as much as I hoped. Just a few photos. Still, never mind. Can't win 'em all.'

Max let that go. 'Did your Aunt Carys work out what you did?'

'She said she knew it was me who took her money and she'd be going to the police. So, I had to get rid of her. Easy, it was. I asked her over to talk about it, even bought her a Maccy D first, said I was sorry and I'd pay it all back, and we went for a walk in the woods. All I had to do was pop her over the head with a branch.'

Still no lights. Max would soon run out of questions.

He said, 'And Ivor – or Maurice, I suppose you called him. What did he do to you?'

Ollie swore again. 'He was going to come in with me, on the new arcade business. He had plenty of cash – made a fortune out of all the old women he conned. Like this one.' He shook Stella's arm hard, cracking her wrist against the wall. 'He had half a dozen old birds on the go. He said he'd be my partner, but he changed his mind when his mother left her money to her sister instead of him. Seems she didn't care much for him.'

Max was glad he couldn't see the expression in Ollie's eyes. The man sounded more unhinged with every word he spoke.

Ollie went on, 'Well, I rang Maurice, all sympathetic about his ma dying. Said we should meet in the woods, see where she died, lay some flowers, all that stuff. What's that thing called? A shrine, that's the word. We were going to make one of those in the woods. Maurice always had a soft spot for his ma. Broke his pathetic little heart when she left home, it did. He kept a photo of her in his pocket and he used to moon over it something dreadful. Sickening, it was.'

He stopped talking for a moment, as though remembering.

'Anyway, where was I? Oh, yes, he was crying, snivelling, going on about his poor mother – and she hadn't even left him her money! I told him, straight out, it was me what topped her.' He whistled. 'Whew, was he mad. Ran at me. I reckon he'd have killed me, except I was quicker than him, see. I'd done it before, hadn't I? Grabbed a dead branch, just like before, and swung it at him. One blow on the side of the head, that's all it took, and that was the end of Cousin Maurice.'

Ollie's teeth gleamed in the darkness. He was laughing. 'Oh, my, what a feeling. Two dead, and all Exham running around, wondering who was sending them nursery rhymes, and what did it all mean? I thought I was going to die laughing, mate, thinking about you and your precious Libby, trying to work out who was sending them. Didn't have a clue, did you? Not so clever as you thought, eh, Ramshore.' Abruptly, the laughter stopped. 'Now, that's enough chat. One of these ladies is going to fly. But which one?'

And then, the floodlights sprang into life on the bridge, high-lighting the four of them in a tableau against the surrounding darkness.

'Is something wrong, here?' A uniformed figure appeared from the toll booth, walking towards the group.

'Keep back!' Ollie leapt up on to the wall, still gripping Stella's arm.

Max hissed at the bridge keeper, 'Don't come too close. He'll throw her over.'

'Keep him talking,' the attendant murmured. He raised his voice against the wind. 'Do you need to talk? Maybe I can help you.'

Ollie laughed, his voice harsh. 'Too late for that.'

Max racked his brains. What to talk about that wouldn't infuriate Ollie further? 'What about Bert? Why's he mixed up with this? How did he get involved?'

'Bert here was going to be a bouncer in the new arcade. Not the sharpest knife in the drawer, our Bert. Useful muscle, though.'

Bert opened his mouth as if about to object to the insult, but Max said, 'Come on, Bert. See sense. We know this is all Ollie's idea. You weren't even there when he hit his aunt, or when he topped his cousin in the woods. He'll be in prison for years for two murders, but you're the junior partner. You haven't killed anyone. They'll let you off lightly if you end all this nonsense.'

It was unlikely, Max knew, but Bert might be convinced.

'I dunno.' The big man looked from Max to Ollie, as if unsure, although he kept his grip on Libby's arm.

The wind dropped, and for a moment, Max thought things would end peacefully. He took a small step forward, but that was too much for Ollie.

He hauled on Stella's arm, forcing her to scramble up with him on the wall as he shouted, 'Shut up, the lot of you. It's time to get rid of one of these tarts. Which one, Max? This one, the old wife? Or the new?'

Libby said. 'The police will know it's you. There's a witness, now.'

Max said, 'Ollie, there's a way out of this. Let the women go and we'll talk about clearing it all up.'

Ollie's voice was shrill. 'Choose, Max, which one?'

For the first time, Stella spoke, her voice soft, but clear. 'Me. Throw me. I don't care.'

Ollie took a half-step back, stunned. 'What?'

'In fact, I'll jump by myself. I tried to end it all last week. I know you didn't believe I meant it, Max, but I did. So, you all stay there and I'll jump.'

'No.' Max and Libby shouted together.

Stella leaned out over the gorge.

'Not yet.' Ollie grabbed at her. 'Not—'

Stella twisted away, Ollie's grip still tight on her arm. For a moment, the pair of them hovered over the edge, suspended between death and safety. But Ollie's momentum took him too far.

He dropped Stella's arm and rocked, flailing, hands grasping at the air, for moments that seemed to Max to last for hours. At last, he lost his balance, and with a scream that echoed around the Avon Gorge, dropped into the darkness below, leaving Stella on her knees on top of the wall, staring down into the abyss.

* * *

Shivering, frightened and suffering from the exhausting after-effects of a monumental adrenalin rush, Max drove with Stella and Libby to the Avon Gorge Hotel, followed by a couple of police officers. Alerted first by the security guard, and then by the bridge keeper, they'd arrived seconds after Ollie had fallen.

The hotel management, gripped by Max's modified version of their adventures on the bridge, offered their best rooms. Max ordered an extravagant amount of room-service food, which they chewed steadily as Libby and Stella recounted their separate stories.

Stella, Max thought, seemed unnaturally calm. Had the stress of watching a man fall to his death been too much for her?

When the police left at last, Libby said, 'For a moment, I thought you'd managed to save Ollie.'

Stella shrugged. 'It was his own fault. He nearly took me with him.'

'You weren't really thinking of jumping, were you?' Libby asked.

Stella just raised one eyebrow.

'Well, he deserved it.' Max was shaking his head. 'I thought he was an old friend. I can hardly believe it. I thought we could talk him down, that he'd see sense. But I was wrong. He was too full of hate. He hated Exham for the way they treated his grandmother, hated Carys and Maurice/Ivor for not helping him out with money, hated you and me, Libby, for putting him out of work.' He shook his head. 'If only he'd come to me, told me he needed a backer. He was my old friend. I would have tried to help.'

Libby said, 'Max, I'm afraid he hated you most of all. I suppose, for your success in life, your money and your big house…'

'And, I'm about to get married to you. Jealousy and hate. He really wanted me to suffer – be reviled, like his grandmother was, even blamed for the murders. He was a sad, twisted man.' He looked at Stella and Libby, so different from each other, both such strong women. 'What about that business with the pills?' he asked Stella. 'Were you faking, then?'

'Well,' she drawled. 'You'll never know that for sure, will you? But it won't happen again.' She shuddered. 'Standing on that wall, looking down into the gorge, taught me a lesson; I'm not ready to go yet. I'm in my prime, like you two. Maybe there's even someone out there for me.' She gave one of her tinkly laughs. 'I'll stick to someone my own age, next time. No more gold-diggers for me. Although, I have to admit, it was fun with Ivor, while it lasted.'

37

AFTERMATH

Libby, exhausted by events, spent the next day with her feet up, recovering. 'I'm going to sit around drinking tea and eating cake. Although,' thinking of the dress hanging on the back of her bedroom door, 'not too much cake.'

'We need a post-mortem,' Max pointed out.

Libby groaned. 'Unfortunate phrase, in the circumstances.'

'Sorry, but everyone in town was so worried when you disappeared, and confused, as well. Mandy, of course, is desperate to know the details. After all, her father's in police custody at the moment.'

'Well, let's ask a few people over. Just Mandy, Robert – he's terribly proud of helping with the family trees – Ali and Angela. They'll be able to pass the facts on to everyone else, and knock any last rumours on the head. I'd rather tell the story once than keep going over bits of it.'

'I'm afraid it's going to be the main topic of conversation in the café for a long while,' Max pointed out. 'Still, let's talk it all through. Drinks at my place?'

'Of course. Bear and Shipley will want to be there.'

Libby's phone rang. Reluctantly, for she longed to sleep, she answered.

'Mrs Forest?' The voice was familiar, but she couldn't put a name to it. 'This is Mary Atkins.'

Atkins, Atkins? Did she know an Atkins? Dazed by yesterday's events, she shook her head. Then, she remembered Mrs Atkins – the woman with five children from the Santa Special, in whom Shipley had taken such an interest. What on earth did she want? Libby had offended her, and the last thing Libby needed now was an argument.

'I'm ringing to thank you. After we spoke about your dog, I began to wonder – you know, I've heard about dogs sniffing out medical problems, and I've been very tired lately, so I went to see Dr Sheffield.'

'You did?'

'Yes, and he was so kind. He thinks I might have something wrong – he doesn't know what, but he's getting me a hospital appointment in less than two weeks.'

Libby hardly knew what to say, but Mrs Atkins was still talking.

'Of course, it's all very worrying, but he said dogs like Shipley have saved people's lives, and he was glad I'd called in, and I just wanted to say thank you, and to apologise for being so rude.'

'No problem at all – it must have sounded so strange to you.' Libby was stammering. 'But I hope whatever it is...' she ran out of words.

Mary Atkins helped her out. 'Whatever it is, I'm better off knowing about it.'

* * *

'And that,' Libby said to Max, as they waited for their friends to arrive that evening, 'means Shipley is a star.'

Mandy arrived first. 'It's quiet in the cottage without you Mrs F,' she said as Libby hugged her. 'I suppose I need to get used to it.' Her face looked paler than ever, but at least she'd dialled down the purple lipstick.

'I miss it a bit, too,' Libby admitted. 'That cooker...'

'Don't pine too much. You'll be back in the New Year, designing new chocolates.' Mandy sighed. 'I've known Dad was a loser for a long time, but I can't believe he's, like, a proper criminal,' she said. 'Mum's pretty upset.'

'Ollie was the real villain,' Max said. 'We were friends at school. He didn't care for much except sports until he discovered computer games. They were unsophisticated, in those days, but it was the start of a golden age for computing and Ollie found he was good at it.'

Libby agreed. 'Meanwhile, Maurice/Ivor was the black sheep of the family. In and out of prison, then preying on older women, conning them into funding a series of a comfortable lives in Surrey.'

'Always thought Surrey was full of shady characters from London,' Mandy put in.

Max laughed. 'Some charmers like Maurice/Ivor have a knack of worming their way into women's lives and cadging money off them, and he was a good-looking guy.'

Libby said, 'That's what he did with Stella?'

'I'm afraid so. She's admitted to giving him expensive presents; that watch he was wearing when I met him at the hospital, for example.'

'Well,' Libby said, 'your ex-wife might be a bit gullible when it comes to toy boys, but she's no wilting flower. She did a great job at the bridge.'

Max said, 'She tells me she's learned her lesson when it comes to men. Not sure I believe her, but so long as she's happy. She's looking out for a decent, kind man of her own age.'

'And no more suicide attempts, either real or manufactured.'

'So she says. Besides, Joe and Claire are planning to keep a close eye on her in future. However, you'll be pleased to know she has no intention of living anywhere near Exham. "Too quiet," she says.'

Angela said, 'I don't understand why Ollie killed Maurice/Ivor. It doesn't make sense to me.'

Libby replied, 'Claire told me that sons very rarely murder their mothers, but aunts are a different matter. Ollie didn't care about Carys. He'd already ingratiated himself with her and used her credit cards. She found out, and threatened to tell the police unless he gave the money back – and if he returned it, he'd be broke again. He was in a dilemma, and that was when he had the idea of killing her. She was happy to walk in the woods with her nephew. He apologised, said he'd pay it all back. And then, the moment she turned away from him, he hit her on the head.'

Mandy was nodding, taking in the details. 'He'd thought the money would go to Maurice/Ivor, but Carys left her money to her sister. I suppose she knew, deep down, that Maurice was a bad lot. That's why Ollie went round to Gladys' shop, wanting to work his charms on her as he had with Carys. Luckily for Gladys, she was away. He lost his temper and trashed the place.'

Robert said, 'Quite a crime spree. But, hold on a minute. You're losing me. That still doesn't explain why he killed Maurice/Ivor. They were on good terms, weren't they?'

Max said, 'He made the mistake of telling Maurice/Ivor what he'd done, not realising his cousin, who he thought of as a hard man, would be shocked and horrified. But Maurice/Ivor had left burglary behind. He'd changed his name and made a new life, even if it was as a con artist. Ollie had already killed once. It had been easy and no one had suspected him. Killing Maurice/Ivor didn't bother him at all, and it meant he wouldn't talk to the police.'

Libby shuddered. 'It's often like that, I've heard. Once you've killed one person, the next is easier.'

Mandy said, 'And my dad got caught up in it all. But why did they send those emails, and kidnap Libby and Stella?'

Max sighed. 'Out of hatred for me, I'm afraid, and for Ramshore and Forest, Private Investigators. I should have realised, when I talked to Ollie that day in Watchet, that he blamed us for putting Pritchards – and him – out of business. He lost his main source of income, his business collapsed, he went bankrupt and his wife left him. He laid all that bad luck at our door. I always thought he was a friend, but he forgot all that. He just wanted to ruin my life, the way he thought I'd ruined his. The emails and the fake social media accounts were all part of his elaborate game. He never grew up beyond playing Dungeons and Dragons, if you ask me.'

'It's an uncomfortable thought – to be hated so much.'

'Joe would say, from a policeman's perspective, it goes with the job. For Ollie, the coincidence of my finding Carys Evans' body hidden in the woods was a gift that gave him the idea for revenge on me that would, at the same time, divert attention from him and the real reason for Carys' death.'

'Nice family,' Mandy said.

Max went on with the story. 'The timing of the emails had puzzled us for a while. Why would the killer send one to Carys when she was already dead? That was a clever move by Ollie. He wasn't stupid, after all. In one stroke, he moved the focus of the investigation to the emails, and began to lay hints that I was the Rhymer. That's why he sent emails to Stella – to point the finger at me. It was a macabre kind of game for Ollie – remember, here was a real-life game all of his own. I bet he followed me to Watchet that day, planning to talk to me, see what I knew. He found I knew nothing. So much for my investigative skills.'

He looked at Mandy. 'Ollie just recruited your father for the kidnap. Bert probably thought it was all a bit of a joke. He's not – well...' he caught a warning glance from Libby, 'let's just say you get your brains from your mother. There's been no love lost between Bert and Libby since the day you and Libby and Bear stopped him attacking your mum. But he was only interested in the kidnap. When he realised Ollie was serious, and about to kill Libby, he was horrified. He's told everything he knows to the police.'

'So, Dad is stupid, rather than wicked? That's something, I suppose. Though, not much.'

Libby was thinking aloud. 'When I was in Bristol, shopping, Bear growled, as though there was someone around he knew was a threat. I reckon that could have been Bert. He lives in Bristol.'

Angela said, 'He won't be living there for a while. Your mum will be relieved, Mandy.'

Libby said, 'So, much of this goes right back to that business with Pritchards. I thought that was finished and all in the past, but the repercussions just keep coming. There are a few people still in prison, and I suppose they won't be there for ever. Should we be worried?'

Max looked grim. 'Unfortunately, Chesterton Wendlebury – one of the directors of Pritchards – is due to leave prison next year.'

Libby gave a little gasp. How would she feel if she saw that man again? She took a steadying breath. 'He wasn't the master-mind of the Pritchards scams. In any case, I don't expect he'll be coming back to Exham any time soon.'

38

The morning of Libby's wedding dawned calm and cold. A watery sun sat low on the horizon, in a sky of startling wintry blue. Libby felt perfectly calm and more relaxed than she would have believed possible.

Yesterday, she'd talked far into the night with Max before he left, determined not to tempt fate by catching sight of the bride on the morning of the wedding. 'Although,' he'd pointed out, 'it's not so much luck we need as a little peace and quiet for a while. Thank goodness my ex-wife is safely back at home in Surrey, where she's apparently become some sort of celebrity, after that business on the bridge.' He'd confessed, 'I thought I was going to lose you, Libby, and if that happened, I don't know what I would do. So, please, take care of yourself. Maybe you could stay indoors for the next year?'

Libby opened her bedroom window a crack. The air was still, the scent of wood fires lingering, as sparrows and goldfinches gathered to feast on fat balls at the bird feeder. Blackbirds hopped across the grass – she couldn't dignify it with the term 'lawn' – pecking for worms. Just as she was about to turn away, a robin alighted on the windowsill, looked her in the eye, and flew into a nearby tree.

Ali, who'd stayed last night, arrived bearing a tray stacked high with toast and marmalade, a pot of tea and a vase of nodding, pink winter hellebores from the garden. 'About the only plants Bear hasn't destroyed.'

Libby's dress hung behind her bedroom door. She'd changed her mind so many times, discarding and returning two dresses she'd bought that weren't quite right. Finally, two days ago, Angela had taken her in hand. Together, they'd scoured Bristol's shops and markets, finally deciding on rose-pink velvet. Ali's gorgeous dark blue, expertly taken in, would complement it beautifully. One day, Libby would get her daughter to teach her to sew.

The tiny wedding Libby and Max had planned had grown out of all recognition. Her dramatic disappearance from the café on the morning it opened had led to the local press interviewing any of her friends they could find. Once the news that she was about to be married became public, she was inundated with phone calls and cards. So many local residents wanted to be at the service that, at Max's suggestion and with Angela's help, they'd managed to book a local hotel for the event.

She spent the morning fidgeting, dressing far too early, pacing through the house, unable to sit for fear of crushing the velvet at the back of her dress. 'After all,' Ali pointed out, 'that's the part everyone will be looking at while you're saying the vows.'

A car drew up outside and Libby threw open the door, to see the orange Jeep from Alan's garage, with Robert at the wheel.

'What's going on?' Libby asked, puzzled. 'Where's your car?'

'This is a wedding present from Max.' Robert frowned. 'He seems to think you'll like it. Can't think why.'

'But I can. I love it. It's perfect. And that's why Alan wouldn't sell it to me.'

Ten minutes later, Libby stood at the entrance to the hotel. Ali stood close behind with Bear and Shipley, both miraculously on their best behaviour. Libby turned and briefly took Ali's hand. 'Thank you for being here. It means so much to me.'

Ali smiled. She'd regained most of her weight, and her cheeks glowed with colour, but a new air of gravity told Libby that her daughter's heart still ached for her lost child.

Robert stood by Libby's side, bursting with pride, ready to walk his mother down the aisle.

Pachelbel's 'Canon in D' swelled as the door opened onto a flower-filled room, abundantly decorated by Gladys. Every seat was full. Libby hadn't realised she had so many friends in Exham.

Her gaze swept over the rows of familiar faces turned towards her. Angela and Owen beamed at her, standing alongside Joe and Claire, while Gemma Humberstone stood next to a bashful PC Tim Green. He ran a nervous finger around his too-tight collar.

The History Society was there in force, clustered together, ranks swelled by new recruits, Jemima, Archie Phillips and Quentin Dobson, with Amy Fisher and her husband close by. As Amy had said, there was nothing she liked more than a wedding where she could watch from the congregation, while the registrar did the work.

As Libby breathed in, ready to begin the walk down the aisle, she caught sight of Annabel, her bored-looking son slouching at her left side. Alan Jenkins stood on her right. What's more, he was holding her hand.

Alan buying chocolates, popping into the bakery and helping to fix the decorations. Annabel visiting the garage – it all made sense, now, but Libby had no time to think about it further, for there, at the end of the aisle, stood Max, the man she knew she had always been destined to marry, smiling at her. She met his eyes and forgot about everyone else.

She laid one hand lightly on her son's arm. 'I thought today would never come,' she murmured in his ear, 'that night on the bridge. But here we are, safe and sound.'

The music rose louder as she stepped forward.

'Nothing can go wrong, now.'

ACKNOWLEDGMENTS

Murder at the Gorge is the seventh book in the Exham on Sea Series. Our friends in the town open a new café during the story, selling Libby's cakes and chocolates and Mandy's scones, but they needed a name for the venture.

I asked members of my VIP club for suggestions, and I was thrill to receive over 100 great ideas.

However, there can only be one winner and one name, so the Exham on Sea café will now be known as *The Crusts and Crumbs Café*.

Peta Ward, who made this brilliant suggestion, points out that detective work involves following the crumbs of clues, and discarding the useless crusts in the way.

Thank you so much, Peta, for thinking of such a terrific name.

Some of the action in *Murder at the Gorge* takes place on the edge of Bristol, where Clifton Suspension Bridge soars over the Avon Gorge, connecting Clifton with North Somerset. Designed by Isambard Kingdom Brunel, it's a tribute to his genius, although he died before it was built.

The view from the bridge is stunning – if you don't mind looking down over 300 feet into the gorge.

Libby and Max also find their way to one of my favourite places, Watchet, a delightful coastal town in West Somerset, where a small chapel sits above a thriving museum, close to the harbour.

I'd like to thank the team at Boldwood Books, especially my editor, Caroline Ridding, for their help in editing and producing this, the seventh Exham on Sea murder mystery, and finally, send a heartfelt thank you to my neighbours in Somerset, none of whom has complained, yet, about the extraordinary number of 'murders' taking place in the area.

MORE FROM FRANCES EVESHAM

We hope you enjoyed reading *Murder at the Gorge*. If you did, please leave a review.

If you'd like to gift a copy, this book is also available as an ebook, digital audio download and audiobook CD.

Sign up to become a Frances Evesham VIP and receive a free copy of the Lazy Gardener's Cheat Sheet. You will also receive news, competitions and updates on future books:

https://bit.ly/FrancesEveshamSignUp

Discover more about the world of Frances Evesham by visiting boldwoodbooks.com/worldoffrancesevesham

ALSO BY FRANCES EVESHAM

The Exham-On-Sea Murder Mysteries

Murder at the Lighthouse

Murder on the Levels

Murder on the Tor

Murder at the Cathedral

Murder at the Bridge

Murder at the Castle

Murder at the Gorge

The Ham Hill Murder Mysteries

A Village Murder

ABOUT THE AUTHOR

Frances Evesham is the author of the hugely successful Exham-on-Sea Murder Mysteries set in her home county of Somerset. In her spare time, she collects poison recipes and other ways of dispatching her unfortunate victims. She likes to cook with a glass of wine in one hand and a bunch of chillies in the other, her head full of murder—fictional only.

Visit Frances's website: www.francesevesham.com

Follow Frances on social media:

facebook.com/frances.evesham.writer
twitter.com/FrancesEvesham
instagram.com/franceevesham
bookbub.com/authors/frances-evesham

ABOUT BOLDWOOD BOOKS

Boldwood Books is a fiction publishing company seeking out the best stories from around the world.

Find out more at www.boldwoodbooks.com

Sign up to the Book and Tonic newsletter for news, offers and competitions from Boldwood Books!

http://www.bit.ly/bookandtonic

We'd love to hear from you, follow us on social media:

 facebook.com/BookandTonic
twitter.com/BoldwoodBooks
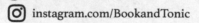 instagram.com/BookandTonic

CPSIA information can be obtained
at www.ICGtesting.com
Printed in the USA
LVHW032300111120
671488LV00016B/1280